T0147193

GOLDS

CONSTANTIN MIC

authorHOUSE®

AuthorHouse™
1663 Liberty Drive
Bloomington, IN 47403
www.authorhouse.com
Phone: 1 (800) 839-8640

Published by AuthorHouse 05/03/2019

ISBN: 978-1-7283-1007-7 (sc)
ISBN: 978-1-7283-1008-4 (e)

CHAPTER

1

It was a warm summer morning. The suns bright rays flooded the room through the silk curtains. A loud groan echoed through the empty apartment as Shade Hunter awoke from his sleep. He yawned as he slowly rubbed his eyes. A smirk slowly came across his lips, he looked at the window and said quietly to himself, "It looks like it will be another beautiful day." Little did he know, that claim wouldn't even begin to describe it. As he sat down in the kitchen to see what there was to eat, he turned on the T.V. to hear the morning news. The same as he did every morning. Most stories were very uninteresting, but one story caught his attention. It said, "The head of the Rags gang, Daniel Lapis, has been apprehended last night. The gang however is not expected to disperse. Police say that even with his capture they will simply elect a new leader. The problem however is with Daniels youngest daughter. The poor girl had no involvement with the mafia however because of her father's position she possesses certain secrets that would make the gang want her dead. The girl however was reported missing after her father went to jail. It is now a race to see who will find her first, the authorities or the Rags gang." Shade didn't know why but that caught his interest. He was also a runaway and couldn't help feeling bad for that girl. If the cops find her, they will interrogate her and send her to an orphanage. Depending which cops catch here they might even hand her over to the Rags. If the actual Rags find her, they would take away her life. He sighed and turned off the T.V. There wasn't time to think about that girl right now. Besides he was an official member of the Gold's. The enemy gang of the Rags. What would they say if he did want to help her? He walked out the door and locked it behind himself, before starting his normal day. Or at least as normal as it gets for an official member of a gang.

CHAPTER

2

Shade slowly ran a hand through his soft brown hair as he walked through a small park on the way home. His posture was slightly slouched showing that he had a hard day. His bright blue eyes seemed almost lifeless as he walked through the park on that warm summer evening. The sun gleamed off the red and black tattoo on his right shoulder. The tattoo was of a red number zero with a black line crossing through it, a tattoo he had since the day he began his involvement with The Gold's. He talked quietly in his normal yet exhausted tone, "Damn Daxyz, why does he give me more work than all the rest of those morons. Ehh but to be fair he does pay me triple than the rest of em, heh." he smirked at his own comment. It had been almost four years since he ran away from home, and four years since he and Daxys first met. Shade didn't particularly enjoy the gang jobs he was given. However, those jobs paid the bills, so he couldn't complain too much. The sky was a reddish gold color as the sun was setting. It seemed quite uneventful until he noticed another person in the park. It was slightly odd since usually nobody goes to this park at this hour. It wasn't exactly a good neighbourhood. He noticed it was a girl as he walked a bit closer in that direction, and not just any girl, a very cute girl. She was sitting on a swing and seemed to be deep in thought. The girl had long blond hair and was wearing very elegant cloths, not the types of cloths you wear in this area. His natural curiosity led him to go over and sit on the swing beside her. "Hello there, fine evening we are having tonight huh?" he said with his usual bright smile. The girl did not respond. She did not even look at him or give even the slightest remark he was there. Her mind seemed to be galaxies away. Several moments passed. Shade tried to begin a conversation again. "Is there something troubling you?" Yet again the girl made no reply. He thought of just leaving but then he heard a loud deep voice calling from somewhere out of sight. "Where'd that little brat go!" called one deep male voice. "That kid is messing with the Rags now!" called a different male voice. Anger and rage were in both their voices. "Crap. This isn't good." said Shade in an unusually calm way for the situation at hand. He figured the Rags had saw him earlier and wanted to pay him back for all he had done that day. He was a Golds member after all, messing with the Rags was in the job description. The reason he was extra tired today was due to messing with some of the local Rags members. He didn't expect to be followed and was ready to run for it but then froze. He turned to look at the girl. He knew if he left her here, dressed as fancy as she was, those Rags would target her for sure. As a gentleman he could not let that happen. The sound of the voices drew nearer and nearer. Nervously Shade looked around. The girl still had not moved or said a word. "How do I get myself out of this one" he muttered quietly.

CHAPTER

3

The voices were drawing nearer and time quickly ticking away. In a moment of panic Shade swiftly grabbed the girls arm and pulled her into a bush where they would be unseen. He whispered softly to her, "Sorry but those guys are bad news. It's safer to just hide out for a bit." The girl still said nothing but now instead of looking down she looked deeply in his eyes. Her expression said calmness but her eyes said Sorrow. He had to look away from her for a brief moment to look out from the cover of their hiding spot. He saw two of the biggest most brutish looking Rags he ever laid eyes on. He knew that people like them only handled the big matters, they couldn't be after him. In his mind he thought, "Could they be after this girl?" He kept a close eye on the Rags until they left the area and their deep roaring voices could no longer be heard. The bush they were hiding behind was very thick but Shade was still relieved they were not seen. With a heavy sigh of relief he turned back to look at the place where the girl had been hiding beside him. "I think it's clea..." he stopped in mid sentence noticing the girl who was once beside him a mere moment ago was gone. "She must have sneaked off when I was keeping watch" he thought to himself. He knew he had to find her before they did. There were some questions he had to ask her. As well there was no way thugs of that class were after him so that only means... He stopped himself mid thought remembering the news article he had seen earlier that day. His eyes widened and he put a hand on his forehead feeling incredibly dumb for not realizing it earlier. He said out loud to himself, "That's the girl from the morning news! Crap I gotta find her before they do!" He ran off in a hurry searching every inch of the park for that girl. It took him a full hour to search every inch of the park. He was now exhausted, not only from searching, but from the whole day of work he had done for the Golds. The sun had completely set and the park was completely dark. The only light that made it slightly easier to see was the incredible full moon out that night. He managed to find his way back to the swing and decided to wait for the street lights to go on. The moon had become engulfed by some clouds making it completely dark now. As he sat in dark silence, suddenly soft sobs were heard in the darkness of the night. The sobs were coming from the swing beside him.

CHAPTER

4

The street lamps finally turned on illuminating the whole park. He could clearly see the girl sitting in the swing beside him and could see the tears pouring down her cheek. Shade spoke softly, "You're the daughter of the old Rags boss aren't you?" Silently she nodded trying to avoid eye contact. Shade let out a heavy sigh. He wanted to help her, he truly did, he knew what it felt like to be an orphan all alone on the streets. But what could he do? She was a Rags, what would Daxys and the others say? No. He had no time for thoughts like that. She wasn't a Rags, she was a girl who needed his help. At that time, he didn't care what would happen to him all he knew was he had to get her to a safe location. Just then he heard the deep howling voices yet again, "Let's check there again and call it a night "the voice barked. Shade was actually thankful that the Rags searching for her were stupid enough to announce where they were heading. Quickly shade took the hand of the girl whose name he did not even know yet and gently pulled her hand as he whispered silently, "Come with me, I'll take you to a safe place for tonight at least." The girl seemed surprised that anyone actually wanted to help her. After the life she had, it was understandable. As well, at the moment Shade grabbed her hand he could have sworn he saw the faintest blush spread across her pale white cheeks. "Stay quiet and don't let go of my hand ok?" he whispered in his softest voice. She looked deeply into his eyes and quickly nodded. They made their way through the park avoiding the sound of the male Rags voices. Shade thought he would try to take her to Daxys safe house and explain the scenario, but the Gold's base was too far away. The streets are crawling with Rags at this hour. He decided he would take her to his home where he was headed in the first place. They walked through the cover of the trees where the street lights barely shined. As they got out of the park Shades apartment building could be seen across The Street. They walked across the empty street and just as thing were looking safe a deep voice called from behind them with the fierceness of roaring thunder, "I see someone! I think it's her!" Shade froze for a brief moment, the only words that could escape his lips were, "Aww damn..."

CHAPTER

5

As the voices drew closer Shade felt as if he was at a dead end, but despite that he still wasn't going to give up. He looked at the girl with very intense look and pointed to his building. "Go in there and wait for me. Don't come out no matter what you hear." The girl had nothing to do other than simply nod and obey his request. It was right after she entered the building that two men came into sight from the park. Guns pointed to Shades head. The first one seemed to know Shade, probably because Shade has been giving the Rags a hard time for quite a while. In a deep voice the Rags male growled the words, "This isn't who we need, this is just a filthy Gold! I'd recognise this punk anywhere!" Shade growled softly under his breath at the man's words. The second Rags said in an even deeper voice, "Oh we'll at least there will one less Gold running around." The second man raised the gun and pointed it at Shades chest. "Any last words Gold?" Shade remained silent. He knew he had about three bullets left in his gun that was hidden in his pants. He was confident he could hit the mark but there were two of them. Even if he hit one the other would shoot him. Plus in the time it took to draw his gun the filthy Rag would have already shot him. "ugh! If I don't think of something this really might be it for me!" he thought to himself. He made up his mind, he would pull out his gun as fast as he could, shot the first Rag, hope the second Rag would miss then finish the second one. He figured his odds of success were about 2%, but it's all he had. He slowly reached for the gun at his side but before he could even grip the hilt of the gun, "BANG!" A loud gunshot was heard. Shade closed his eyes thinking it was over. A second shot was heard. Several seconds passed but Shade did not feel the piercing pain of the bullet. He opened his eyes and saw both Rags dead on the ground. Quickly he looked back at the building. There was nobody out on any of the balconies, the only person in sight was the mystery girl peeking at him through the door of the building. He smirked as he realized that yet again, he had lucked out. Also he knew who he owed a thank you too. Shade walked towards the girl and said "I thought I told you to hide." As he walked into the building, he could have sworn that for a brief moment he actually saw a smile come across the girls lips. Shade led the way to his apartment and opened the door inviting her in. "Make yourself comfortable, tomorrow I can take you to the Gold's place and I'm sure they will be able to help. And if they can't I'll make them help." Said Shade. The girl just stood there, her expression was still blank but her eyes seemed to no longer be filled with as much sorrow. "Well we better get some rest, I have a feeling tomorrow will be another exciting day" he said with a bright smile. Little did he know that yet again the word "exciting" wouldn't even begin to describe it.

CHAPTER

6

Shade had given the girl his bed and he himself was sleeping on an air mattress in the living room. While he laid there unable to fall asleep, he began to think if maybe he was doing too much for this girl. He did not even know her name. The clouds that had engulfed the moon earlier had dispersed and bright moon light flooded the apartment. He then started to remember the day that he ran away, and what he would have done if Daxys hadn't had helped him. This made him remember why he was doing what he was doing. He had no regrets about what he was doing. After hours of laying awake restlessly he finally managed to drift off to sleep. Meanwhile in his room where the girl was in an uneasy sleep a soft gasp was heard as she awoke. The nightmares she has been having lately came again. She dreamed that she was all alone and that the Rags were after her. In her dream no matter how much she called for help not a single person would help her. She got off the bed and stood there looking down at her feet. She slowly begun to walk to where Shade was sleeping on his air mattress. The rest of the night was completely silent. The next morning Shade woke up with a yawn. He could feel that there was something cuddling up against him, he wondered what the strange soft feeling pressing up against him was. He turned to glance at his side, still half asleep. With wide eyes he looked beside him to see none other than the mystery girl! "w..what?!" He blurted out from the shock. His cheeks blushed darkly due to the sheer fact that he wasn't even fully dressed. The girl woke up hearing his voice and smiled softly looking at him. Her beautiful blue eyes seemed to sparkle. Shade could not help but blush from how incredibly adorable she was and from how close she was to him. "Why are..." Shade was interrupted by a loud bang on the door. A deep roaring voice echoed from the door. "We know she is in there! Open up!" The voice roared. "Crap they found us already?!" Shade thought to himself. "Open up and give her to us easily! If you do maybe we won't kill you!" the roaring voice echoed. Shade looked at the girl and saw her eyes were now filled with fear. He had to think fast of how to get out of this one. He looked around franticly and got an idea. "Aha! I know!" He blurted out.

CHAPTER

7

The sound of fists pounding against the door echoed throughout the entire apartment. The girl looked around frantically not knowing what to do. Should she give herself up? At least that way Shade would be spared. Or at least that's what the Rags said. Her eyes quickly filled with tears at the thought of the only person who ever helped her dying because of her. She looked beside her to see Shade was already fully dressed. "Keep quiet and come on" He took her hand and gently pulled her to the balcony. She couldn't help but blush as Shade took her hand. She blushed even more due to the fact that even though Shade had changed she was still in an extra-large shirt Shade had given her to wear for the night. They stepped out on the balcony and Shade quickly jumped on the ledge. The eyes of the girl widened. She didn't know what the heck he was doing. He took a deep breath and jumped straight down. The girl let out a high-pitched scream as she ran to the side of the balcony to see if he killed himself. However instead of seeing a lifeless corpse on the floor she saw nothing. What had happened to him? This all felt like a horrible nightmare. A crack sound was heard from inside the apartment signalling that the door was almost broken down. Tears poured down her face as she began to lose all hope. But then, in the middle of all her panic a soft calming voice was heard. Her tears stopped as she heard the voice, she knew that voice, it was Shades voice?! She looked over the edge of the balcony once again to see none other than Shade wavering at her from the balcony bellow the one she was in. "Alright it's your turn, jump!" he said to her. His voice was very calm as if jumping from balconies was second nature. She couldn't believe what he was asking and how calmly he was asking it. What if she didn't land on the balcony ledge? They were pretty high up after all, the fall would kill her. Shades soft calm voice spoke again. "We don't have much time, trust me, just jump. "She noticed the ledge of the balcony bellow was quite a bit wider than the ledge of Shades balcony. That's probably how he got down so easily. However, there was still a chance she might fall. She heard the sound of the door breaking down. Shade voice came again "Hurry! It's now or never!" She closed her and decided to trust him. She climbed on the ledge as the wind blew through her soft blonde hair. Without another thought she jumped. She landed on the ledge of the lower balcony with merely her heels. However, she did not have enough balance. She could feel herself falling backwards. Panic flooded her mind and it seemed as if the entire world was in slow motion as she fell back. Suddenly she could feel a hand grab hers. It pulled her back from the ledge. Instead of falling off the balcony she fell into the balcony. Her eyes were closed from the fear but she could feel that she had landed on something warm. She opened her eyes and blushed crimson red when she noticed that she had fallen right on top of Shade. Their faces were only mere inches apart. He looked deeply into her eyes as she looked back into his. Still blushing crimson red, she slowly moved her lips closer to his. Her lips were a mere fraction of an inch away. However, in that moment she heard the door to the balcony they had landed on open. The cocking of a shotgun echoed as an unfamiliar voice growled the words "Who the hell are you?"

CHAPTER

8

The girls eyes widened as she stared into the barrel of the shot gun. The man who stood over them was a tall skinny Russian man, he had short black hair and pale skin. In the middle of her fear Shades calming voice was heard once again. "You really know how to kill a moment Albert" Shade spoke in a slightly annoyed voice. The man looked at Shade and chuckled. "Oh I should have guessed it was you, what do you need this time?" Albert said with a soft smile as he lowered his shotgun. As both Shade and the girl stood up she noticed that the man actually looked not much older than Shade. "Well you see..." Shade began to say but was interrupted by Albert "That girl, she isn't who I think she is, is she?" Hearing his words the girl looked down shyly at her feet. Shade knew that Albert must have seen the same news article as he had seen the other day. "Yes." Shade said in a calm yet firm tone. "Hmm, and judging by the noise upstairs you need help again, right?" Said Albert in the same calm tone. "I want to get her to Daxys place, I figured he could handle the rest." Said Shade. As he spoke loud footsteps could be heard in the apartment above them. "Oh, and some of the Rags top dogs are after her." Said Shade in still a calm tone. As the girl looked at them and listened to them speak, she could not understand how they were so calm, this scenario would make any normal person stressed beyond belief. It was clear neither Shade nor Albert were normal people. "Ugh... Well let's just say you owe me another one." Said Albert said with a soft sigh as he took his car keys off his desk and handed them to Shade. "I'll handle the guys upstairs, you take my car and get that girl to Daxys." Albert said in a slightly more serious tone. Shade nodded and took the girls hand in his. He pulled her through Albert's messy apartment to the door. The girl blushed slightly, it was the first time she noticed how much bigger Shades hand was then hers. As Shade clenched the door knob and was about to open the door, Albert spoke one more time. "By the way, scratch my car and I swear to god Shade it will seem as though the two morons upstairs got off easy." Albert smirked looking at Shade and the girl. Shade chuckled "Don't worry bro, and thanks again." And without another word Shade and the girl dashed down the hallway towards the stairs. They ran down the stairs, the girl couldn't help noticing how nice and clean the building was, certainly not the kind of place a gangster would be living in. As they walked out into the parking lot the girl noticed how grey rain clouds were starting to fill the previously clear sky. Albert's black minivan was visible not far from where they stood. Compared to the other normal cars Albert's van stuck out like a sore thumb. They got into the van and Shade couldn't help noticing how nervous the girl looked. He looked into her eyes softly and gave her a comforting smile to calm her down. Shade put the keys into the ignition and turned the car on. A loud growling sound was heard from the engine as the car failed to start. Shades smile faded quickly. At that moment several loud gun shots were heard coming from the direction of Shades apartment. Shade clenched the steering wheel with one hand as he kept trying to start the car with the other. The girl looked towards Shades apartment, her heart was racing as she wondered what happened to the man who had helped her and Shade. A small tear poured down her cheek as she sat there helplessly. She thought about how all these people she had just met were protecting her. She wished she could do more than just watch.

CHAPTER

9

The engine roared and the car finally started, an almost sinister smirk spread across Shades lips as if he had just won a battle against the car itself. "Ha! There we go I finally got this old piece of crap to start," he chuckled softly at his own words and turned to look at the girl beside him with a big smile on his face. Shades expression then dropped when he saw hers. "Hey what is it? I got the car started its all okay," he was not exactly sure what she looked so worried about so he just assumed she was frightened by the car not starting. The girl shook her head. Yes she was worried when the car wouldn't start but what she really felt terrible about was when she heard the gun shots and thought Albert may have died trying to help her. She knew however that Shade probably wouldn't be able to guess that's what she was thinking. Therefore, even though she had not spoken a word in quite a while due to the shock of her father being incarcerated, she wanted to explain herself to Shade. She wanted to tell him how sorry she was that his friend could have died protecting her, a girl he had barely just met. She parted her lips slightly and it seemed as though she could barely even make the slightest of sounds but was determined to say what she wanted to say no matter what. "... ... ... I ..." The girl seemed as though she would finally start to speak when once again a loud barrage of machine gun fire was heard. This time it seemed much louder. It seemed as though the shooting took place over a longer time then the first shooting, which she had heard mere moments ago. Shade seemed to have not heard her try to speak due to the loud shooting that had just taken place. "Damn Albert I said get rid of them I didn't say go bat crap crazy... Geez..." Said Shade with a slight sigh in his voice. He then turned to the girl and spoke with a soft smile across his lips, "If it's Albert your worried about don't be. The only people you should worry about are the poor Rags who decided to mess with the wrong Russian weapons expert." Shade chuckled softly and noticed that his comment made her look slightly less worried, however she still seemed deep in thought. "And besides..." continued Shade, in a more serious tone, "Albert wasn't forced to do anything he didn't want to do. He may have seemed like a bit of a jerk but trust me, if I didn't ask him for help he would have done what he is doing now anyway. So no more looking all sad and stuff alright? Life is short and there just isn't any time to feel down about stuff like that. Try smiling once in a while, you look cuter when you do." He gave her a quick wink and shifted the gear shift out of park, pulling the car out of the parking lot and starting to drive down the road. The girl was at a loss for words, despite the fact that she never spoke. She didn't even know what to think, it's as though Shade knew exactly what she needed to hear and said it all while smiling. The girls cheeks were blushing quite red. As they drove down the road to wherever Shade was taking her, his words were the only things on her mind. Her cheeks seemed to get even redder the more she thought about it. Then without any particular reason, she looked at Shade, who's eyes were focused on the road, and gave him a great big smile.

CHAPTER

10

The girl was just sitting in the passenger seat looking out the window, she did not know where she was. When her dad was around he would always take her on drives and they would just talk. Despite being the head of a gang, her father really wasn't that bad of a person. The Rags control a lot of places in this town and she was quite familiar with most of them. That is why she was a bit surprised that she did not have the slightest clue where she was at the moment. They drove down a pretty busy street and took a turn onto one that was completely empty. It was as though nobody else even knew that road was there. There were no cars parked on the edge of the road and no cars going up or down the road. It was slightly peculiar but the girl paid little attention to that fact. There was just grass and a tree on the side of the road, not even any other houses. They drove down that road for a short while, during that time neither of them said anything. Finally, Shade broke the silence, "we are almost there but before we get there you should know, Albert will seem like the most normal compared to the others." The girl was not sure if he was joking or being serious so she just nodded quietly to his comment. They drove until the road finally came to an end. A grand and immense house was at the end of the road. It looked simply exquisite and she was sure the owner must be someone truly praiseworthy to maintain a house like that. They got out of the car and slowly walked to the front door. There was a small speaker at the top of the door. Shades usual smile was spread across his lips but he somehow seemed nervous. He didn't seem as calm and collected as always, she wondered what could be inside that house to make even Shade nervous. Finally, Shade clenched his fist banged on the door. A loud static noise was heard from the speaker at the top of the door. A voice then spoke, "Yea?" The static interfered a lot so it was hard to tell whether the voice was male or female, what was clear however was that the voice didn't care much for visitors. Shade still seeming a bit nervous spoke back, "Its Shade, I want to talk with..." Shade was interrupted by the loud static filled speaker. The voice seemed completely different from a moment ago as if Shade was just the person they wanted to hear from. "Shade! Wait right there I'll come to the door right now!" The girl beside Shade seemed a bit puzzled, she really could not even guess what would happen next. "Oh god..." mumbled Shade placing a palm over his forehead. Unlike the girl beside him it seemed as though he knew exactly what was about to happen. Several brief moments passed and the door wildly swung open. Then without even the slightest warning a girl about the same age as Shade pounced on him like a wild tiger. Her feet were completely off the ground when she bumped into him and quickly wrapped her arms around his neck. The impact made Shade lose his balance and he fell backwards hitting the ground hard with the girl who still held onto him tightly laying right on top of him. Shade groaned in quite a bit of pain from hitting the ground so hard. "Agh Damn it Bia do you have to do this every single time I come here?" Bianca didn't listen to him and just buried her face in his chest. She seemed very much like a cute little puppy who just saw its master for the first time in a while. "You're so mean Shade! You don't call you don't text I was starting to think you didn't like me anymore" She pretended to pout cutely but there was just something very sinister about her expression. The girl who came here with Shade could barely believe her eyes. She didn't know why but she felt a very strong grudge against the girl laying on top of Shade right now. She blushed crimson red and could not understand why she was so jealous of another girl so close to Shade. Bia noticed the other girl standing there and without getting off of Shade she spoke in a quite cynical tone this time, "hey who is that little piece of eye candy there Shade? Don't tell me your cheating on me." Shade cringed when he heard her words, his tone was just as cynical as hers when he responded, "Yea like hell I am, now get off." Bia once again seemed to not even pay attention to his words. "So Shade what are you going to talk with my big bro about? It wouldn't have anything to do with..." She was interrupted by a deep male voice coming from the wide opened door to the house. "Shade... mind telling me what the hell you're doing on the ground with my sister on top of you?" said Daxys, the leader of the Golds gang.

CHAPTER

11

A moment passed where nobody said anything. After a short pause Bia quickly got off Shade and ran behind her big brother, her eyes filled with tears. "Oh big brother I'm so glad you came! Shade forced me down! I told him that his actions were immoral but he wouldn't listen!" Bia tried to sound as sincere as possible. Shade got to his feet without even the slightest trace of emotion on his face. "Yea because that's exactly why you were on top of me, nice try though." Bia who seemed sincerely sad a mere moment ago then smirked sinisterly and spoke in an obviously fake sweet and innocent voice. "You're no fun Shade, I wanted to see how that scenario would have played out." She giggled cutely and then said, "Anyway I'll let you two boys talk about whatever it is you gotta talk about, I'll drop by later tonight Shade" She gave him a wink and then walked away. The girl that Shade had brought with him was even more confused then she had been yet. She now understood why Shade told her that the people in this house would be quite the characters. Daxys took one quick look at the girl Shade had brought with him and raised an eyebrow. "Oh god Shade out of all the people you could have brought with you it just had to be her huh?" When Daxys spoke those words the girl he was referring to took a small step back. Shade looked at him with a quite serious expression. "You know her father is no longer in charge of the Rags. If I didn't help her you know what they would have done to her." Daxys then sighed and raised his palm up to Shade as if asking him to not speak anymore. "Bring her in, we can talk later, I'll get her an extra room for now." Shade then smiled and nodded at Daxys. "Thanks man," he said softly. Shade then turned to the girl and spoke softly "he is going to help us now so you don't have to worry about anything anymore alright? Just relax a bit for now." The girl then nodded slowly. Another member of the gang who was also staying at Daxys place came and showed her to a empty room. Shade stayed behind however and looked at Daxys with an slightly more serious look. Daxys then chuckled and said, "Damn I haven't seen you this serious in a while, what don't tell me you like this girl that much?" Shade's expression then changed to one of shock, the whole serious mood seemed to have flashed away after that one mere comment. Shade then chuckled as well. "Yea I guess I do, I had to go through the same thing she had to go through remember? You're the one who helped me so now I'm going to be the one to help her." Daxys then nodded at Shades comment and spoke softly, "Go to the roof where we usually chat, I'll be there in a minute." Shade then nodded and Daxys went off to most likely finish what he was doing before Shade had showed up.

CHAPTER

12

Shade walked to the second floor of the house. He knew this house far too well. He then pulled down a ladder that led to the attic and climbed up it. When he climbed up into the attic and turned on the lights he looked around. There was a tiny bed in one corner and a desk with a tiny lantern beside it in the other corner. That's all that was up in the attic. Shades memory drifted back to when he had left home. This was the only room Daxys could spare at the time. Shade came from a very high class family. However he just never was that type of person. That life may be for some but it was not for him. He tried talking to his parents but they just ignored him and told him he better be on his best behaviour. The only reason Shade didn't run away sooner was that he cared to much for his younger sister. His father was running for some kind of office political position at one point and after that he didn't even see his parents more than once every other week. He thought that this was not that bad actually. He thought he would finally have some freedom, but he was oh so wrong. His father thought that if he did anything it would reflect on him so he hired that strictest and most formal care givers to take care of him. At one point he wouldn't even be able to see his sister, the only thing keeping him from leaving. That's when he had enough. He packed up whatever he could one night and snuck his way out at around 3 am when the care givers were asleep. He didn't have any plans back then, he is more of the "let's see where this goes" type of person. This was quite a long time ago. Shade was only 16 years old when he ran off on his own. He spent several days on his own. Fall was quickly ending and it was starting to get cold. At the time he thought of returning home and trying again in the spring. As he was just killing sometime swinging on a swing set in the park he saw a group of guys all gathering around a girl. He put his feet down on the ground and stopped swinging, watching closely to see what would happen. They were only one hundred meters away so he couldn't see what exactly was happening but he defiantly saw that the girl did not want those guys crowding around her. He got up off the swing set and walked over to the group of guys crowding the girl and said "Is there a problem here?" The girl as soon as she saw him jumped at the chance and ran beside Shade wrapping both her arms around his right arm. "This is my boyfriend, I told you I have one now go away." She said that in a very annoyed tone, Shade knew that they were harassing her and she was most likely using him as an excuse to get them away. The guys seeing Shade decided to give up on that girl and they all walked away. The girl he had just saved let go of his arm at that point and looked at him with a big smile, she then said, "Sorry about that but those morons were just not leaving me alone, my names Bianca, you can just call me Bia. Thanks for the help!" Shade then smiled back and introduced himself as well. Bia then invited him to her house to thank him for helping her out, that's when he first met Daxys. At first Daxys didn't like Shade, but then again it was only because Bia brought him home and he was always an extremely over protective big brother. That's when Shade found out about the gang "The Golds" that Daxys was in charge of. Daxys said if Shade ever needed a job to get some quick coin, he should just drop by. Daxys even asked where Shade lived, that if he ever needed a ride Daxys could pick him up before a job. Shade however changed the topic quickly every time Daxys brought up the question of where he lived. He did this most likely because at the time he did not have a place to live. They all talked and became decently close but at one point Shade noticed the time. He felt so grateful to the people who took him in for a bit but didn't want to push himself on them. So, he said his goodbyes to them and then left. Daxys had earlier given him a card with his number to call him if he ever needed a job. After Shade was gone Daxys noticed the card on the table they were all sitting at and thought

Shade must have forgotten it. So, he quickly put on a jacket and ran after Shade. Daxys ran after Shade and called his name several times but Shade did not seem to notice. Daxys then thought something seemed a bit off, he didn't know why but for some reason he wanted to see where Shade lived. Shade always avoided the question so Daxys thought he would just find out himself. At first, he was a bit paranoid that Shade may be a Rags spy and lives somewhere in the Rags area. That would explain why he was so opposed to saying where he lived. Daxys followed him at a distance but made sure Shade wouldn't see him. Finally, Shade walked into a park, Daxys was still following him hiding behind the trunk of a big oak tree. Shade then went and sat on a swing in the park. Quite some time passed. The night seemed colder then usual. Daxys could hear Shade mumble to himself, "Damn... It's the coldest night yet..." Daxys didn't know what was going on. Why was that kid sitting on a swing in the cold in the middle of the night? He gave it several more minutes to see if someone would pick him up or if he would go to his home. Nothing happened, it was just a still silence. Nobody came and Shade went nowhere. Shades breath was visible each time he exhaled. Daxys sighed to himself releasing that this kid didn't have a place to stay. He then remembered how this was the same park in which he helped Bia. Shade didn't pass by this park by coincidence when he helped Bia, he seemed to be living here. Daxys then walked up to Shade not hiding any more. "So you need a place to crash?" Daxys said as he sat down on the swing beside Shade. Shade surprised turned his head and saw Daxys sitting beside him. "D...Daxys? What? How did you know I was here?" Daxys pulled out the card he wanted to give Shade and handed it to him. "You're free to stay at my place. It's the least I can do after you helped out my sister." Shade looked at him with a shocked expression not knowing what to say. "Hey don't think this is a freebie though, you better help me out when I got a job for you. Got it? And you won't make that much cash either. If that's alright with you then hurry up and let's go before you catch a damn cold." Daxys got up after saying that and looked at Shade to see if he would come along. "I owe you one man." Shade thought to himself as he got up and started walking with Daxys back to his new home.

CHAPTER

13

Shade was still standing in the attic his memories still flowing back to him. Daxys finally walked up to the attic and stood beside Shade speaking calmly. "You like seeing the place you used to live in huh? It's not that long ago that you saved up enough to get your own place." Shade chuckled and then responded, "Oh the stories this room could tell eh? But the past is over, the present is what we have to focus on. Remember a while back, in the middle of the night you saved that stupid 16 year old kid who couldn't even respond to you when you first offered to help him? Well history repeats its self, only now I'm the one who is going to help that girl. It's funny how things play out isn't it?" Daxys chuckled at that comment and then said, "You don't say eh? Well what were you thinking we could pull off?" Shade then replied, "Let's go to the roof first, for old time's sake?" Daxys smiled and nodded. They opened up the only attic window and they both climbed out on the ledge of Daxys house. They then made their way onto the side of the roof facing the background of Daxys house. Since his house was located where the road stopped there was nothing but trees and beautiful nature scenery. The roof was on a slant just enough that they could lay back on it without falling off. Shade closed his eyes for a couple moments enjoy the peacefulness. However, he knew it wouldn't last long. It rarely does when your part of a gang, but that's what makes life so much fun. Shade then began to speak without opening his eyes. "Do you think maybe she could be part of the Golds? It's what I did when you helped me out." Daxys didn't reply right away but then said, "Do you really think she would be able to do the same things we do? You were within an inch of your life at least twice already this month. I knew from the start that you could pull off high risk situations if you try but do you think she could?" Shade shook his head and replied, "Of course I didn't mean anything dangerous like I do, I just thought that… I don't know she knows a lot of things about the Rags, it's why they want to kill her. Maybe she could help by telling us the things she knows. Maybe with her help we can finally end the conflict with the Rags. In our area at least." Daxys thought again for several moments and then spoke. "That's not a bad idea. All throughout the country the Rags have been slowly dying down. They use to have 7 major bases and 13 minor ones, however now they only have 4 major bases and 8 minor ones. We Golds are slightly higher at 5 major bases and 11 smaller ones. Mine here being one of the minor ones. If we can take out the minor Rags base that is fighting against us here, we can take full control of this area and expand to a major base. Putting us in a better position to finally take them out completely." Shade nodded thinking this is a good plan, he didn't really care about that though all he wanted to do was help the girl he rescued. "Only problem is that girl doesn't talk much. Or well not at all I should say." Said Shade quietly. "Don't worry about it, after the drama she went through it's not something unusual. Give her a couple days at most I'm sure she will talk eventually" replied Daxys. Shade nodded once more. Daxys was quite for a moment but then spoke, "Oh one more thing Shade, do you even know that girls name?" Shades face went completely blank for a moment. He thought about it but realized he did not at any point pick up the girls name. He placed a palm over his face feeling like a complete idiot. "Well in my defence she never spoke a word!" Daxys just burst out laughing, he laughed so hard he actually felt tears coming from his eye. "You'll never change will you Shade?" Said Daxys still laughing at Shade before he spoke again. "Seriously what would you do without me man? Her name is Nemi Lapis. Try not forgetting that too quickly. Its been all over the news." They kept talking about unrelated things for quite a while. It was already night at that point and it was starting to feel cold outside. They both decided to go down stairs and hit the hay for the night. Daxys told Shade one last thing before they left the roof however. "Oh by the way when you see Nemi try to see if she has some kind of tracker on her, if she was the ex leaders daughter I wouldn't be surprised if she had some kind of tracker on her. Gang leaders usually like to keep a close eye on their loved ones. However since the leader is no longer in charge the ones that are after her could use that tracker to find her. You understand what I mean?" Shade nodded.

CHAPTER

14

Shade thought that Daxys may have been a bit paranoid, he couldn't imagine someone doing that just to keep track of their daughter. That would be major over kill. He went to an empty guest room Daxys gave him and even borrowed a loose shirt to wear to sleep. In a way he kind of regretted not asking Daxys to let him crash in his old room. The moon was out again and it flooded his room with light. He tried to sleep but just couldn't no matter how hard he tried. He kept thinking that he should have gone to check on Nemi. However, he also thought she may have already fallen asleep by the time his chat with Daxys ended. He thought he could just talk to her in the morning and apologise for not checking on her the day before. He laid there in his bed for several more minutes until he heard his door slowly creak open. He assumed Daxys forgot to tell him something. However to his biggest surprise when the door was opened Nemi stood there. She was wearing a set of pink pyjamas which made her look even cuter then she usually does. His eyes also caught a silver bracelet on her hand with a Lapis stone pendant attached to it. Shade got up from his bed and looked at her before speaking, stuttering slightly, "Y...Yes? Do you need something?" He didn't really know what he was supposed to say. Nemi walked beside him and sat beside him on his bed. She then looked down and with the quietest yet sweetest voice she spoke the words, "T... Thank you..." Shade was even more surprised now that he got to hear her voice for the first time. Nemi continued speaking, "I don't know why you decided to help me… But thank you for everything you did. I was so depressed when I went to that park that night. I didn't even care if they found me, I was so scared and so alone. But then I met you, you helped without even knowing me. You even got your friends to help me too. I don't know why though but the way you act… your calm way of acting, I just don't feel that scared anymore." After saying everything she wanted, she took a deep breath since she did not even pause for air while speaking. She didn't look Shade in the eyes because she was too embarrassed by what she had just said. Her cheeks were blushing crimson red. Shade was still stunned for several moments but then a warm smile came across his lips, he then spoke in a gentle tone "You don't have to thank me. I did what I did because I wanted to, nothing else. I'm just glad that I could make you feel a bit better." She nodded after hearing this. "You're just too kind Shade." Said Nemi in a soft tone. Shade smiled, "You should get some rest now, I'm sure you must be tired after the long day we had." Nemi said nothing as she just leaned against Shades shoulder. She then spoke silently and very shyly. "Would it be okay if I… stayed with you tonight? I just really don't want to be alone." Shade blushed darkly when he thought about sleeping in the same bed as her. Especially since she was even cuter than usual in her pink pyjamas. As well the fact her voice was so sweet made it impossible to say no. Shade then sighed and said, "Of course you can." Nemi smiled and laid back on Shades bed, however to her surprise Shade then stood up. She didn't really understand what he was doing. Shade open a nearby closet and pulled out two extra blankets and another pillow. Shade then spoke in his usual tone as he was placing one blanket on the ground beside the bed. "Im going to hate mysef for this. But I can't be trusted to sleep beside you." He laid down on the blanket and put the pillow where his head would be. He then covered himself with the second blanket. Nemi was so confused at his actions. She then giggled softly to herself and laid back in the bed whispering softly to herself, "I didn't know guys as nice as him even existed." The moonlight slowly faded as clouds engulfed the moon. The room was now completely dark as they both slowly drifted to sleep.

CHAPTER

15

The sound of rain drops hitting the window could be heard. It seems as though there was a rain storm outside. Shade slowly opened his eyes and yawned as he glanced towards a clock on the wall in front of him. It was around ten o'clock in the morning. Shade glanced at the bed he was laying beside and noticed it was empty. He got up quickly feeling a bit worried wondering where Nemi could have gone. He was distracted however by an amazing smell that seemed to be coming from somewhere. He walks up to the closed door about to place his hand on the door knob when suddenly the door flung open. Shade jumped back a bit surprised but dropped his guard when he saw the person who opened the door. It was just Bia. Bia was wearing an extra large white shirt and a pair of shorts. Her hair was also pretty messy. It was clear she had not woken up until recently either. Shade smiled softly and looked at her as he said, "yes?" Bia walked up to him and pushed him back towards the bed as she sat on it herself. "Sooo?" Bia smirked sinisterly, "How was it? Did you kids have fun last night?" Shades smile then dropped as he sat down beside her placing a palm over his face. "I'm guessing you had something to do with this?" He said as he removed his palm from his face and sat down beside Bia. "Heh who do you think pushed that shy girl to do something so spontaneous, and those pink pyjamas I gave her as well, I know you have a thing for girls in pink." Shade then spoke softly, In his mind Shade disagreed with the shy comment, this was the second time Nemi had done something like sneak into his room at night. Bia pouted seeing Shade was in thought and not replying so she spoke again, "come on tell me how it went! We are best friends for crying out loud. And don't skip the details." Shade sighed knowing what Bia assumed happened last night. Despite how they act around each other it's true that Bia was one of his closest friends so he told her everything about the night before. He specifically mentioned that they did not do anything and that he slept on the floor while Nemi slept in the bed. Bia tried to keep a straight face for as long as she could after hearing his story but then broke out in laughter. "Ha ha! No way! Oh gosh I knew you were that type of guy but didn't imagine you would give up an opportunity as perfect as that one." Shade chuckled, "Yea yea I'm an idiot I know that." Bia giggled a bit but then her expression turned quite serious. Usually when her mood is like that she is just messing with Shade, just like she had done the other day when he first arrived. However, for some reason her mood seemed genuinely serious. She looked away from Shade trying to not make direct eye contact as she spoke in an unusually calm tone for her. "So do you love that girl? Are you two serious?" Bia said quietly. Shade was a bit shocked at that question. He stuttered a bit but replied, "N...No of course not! You always assume things like that Bia, She is in the same scenario I was in when you and Daxys helped me. That's why I'm helping her." Bia's eyes seem to sparkle when she heard those words. She then looked up at Shade, scotched a bit closer to him and said, "Oh so you don't have a girlfriend still is what you're saying?" Shade blushed slightly not knowing where this was going. He could usually tell when Bia was acting but he just didn't sense she was this time. Bia then blushed as well and looked down once more as she spoke, "You know ever since you moved out we haven't seen each other that much. I really do miss you, we give each other a hard time but you know I'm just joking right?" Shade looked at her with a serious yet kind look. "Of course I know that, you don't even have to tell me. Where is this all coming from?" Said Shade. Bia then smiled softly and after a short pause she spoke, "So hey, if you're not dating that Nemi girl do you think... Maybe we could give it a try?" Shade was shocked at what Bia was saying. He was so surprised he just assumed that Bia was messing with him. After several moments of silence he spoke in a non serious tone now, "Yea yea your just messing with me, very funny, I gotta say I almost fell for it this time." Bia was quite for several moments after that. She was looking down so Shade could not tell her emotion very clearly. After several more moments Bia looked up at him with a big smile on her face. She giggled and then said, "Yea you caught me, I was just kidding around haha, of course I was just kidding around. Darn and I was really trying my best acting haha." Bia giggled a bit more and then stood up. She then said, "Anyway I'm going to go down and get some breakfast, talk to you later." Without another word Bia left the room closing the door quickly behind her. Shade was still a bit confused but decided that it was Bia so there was no way she was serious. He laid back on the bed and relaxed for a bit. His back hurt from the floor so he laid there a bit. Bia however after leaving the room and closing the door was still there. She laid back against the door looking down at the floor. There were tears in her eyes. As she stood there, she closed her eyes and very quietly, so to not be heard, she mumbled the word, "Idiot..."

CHAPTER

16

Shade was laying on the bed which was far more comfortable then the hard floor he had slept on. He was thinking about the strange talk he had just had with Bia. He was not sure but for some reason thought that Bia may have romantic feelings for him. Bia messed with him enough times for him to know that something was a bit off this time. However, she admitted at the very end of their chat that she was joking. Shade sighed and thought that maybe she was just getting better at acting or that with all that happened recently he was just reading too much into things. Bia was his very close friend for a long time and that's all. Or at least that's what he convinced himself. He then noticed the great smell coming from the hall way again. "Oh right I was gonna check it out before Bia came in." he mumbled to himself as he stood up from the bed. He then changed into the same cloths he wore yesterday since he had nothing else to wear. When he was fully changed he folded up the extra blankets he had slept on the night before. He than opened the door to his room and walked down the hall way. As he had assumed the smell was coming from the kitchen. However, to his surprise he saw Nemi, wearing a rather cute outfit he assumed she had gotten from Bia. She was standing beside the stove and flipping a pancake. He then glanced at the kitchen table that was full of empty plates covered in maple syrup. He assumed everyone must have had already eaten and gone to do whatever they had to do. Nemi was still making more pancakes however, she was actually so concentrated on the pancakes she did not even notice Shade standing merely several feet behind her. Shade then smiled and spoke in a gentle tone. "Good morning." He said with a bright smile spread across his lips. Nemi did not expect to suddenly hear Shades voice and jumped a bit, she was holding on to the pan and the pancake almost fell off of it when she had jumped. She then put the pan down and turned around, her cheeks blushing slightly red embarrassed that she had jumped like that. She then mumbled silently but cutely, "Oh good morning Shade, I umm was making pancakes for everyone, would you like some too?" Shade was not really used to hearing her talk since she was so quite until the night before. Shade did not reply right away so Nemi then spoke again, "Oh if you don't like pancakes it's okay you don't have to eat them." Shade then smiled and spoke, "No of course I like pancakes, especially if you made them." Nemi then blushed. Suddenly they could hear the sound of a deep male voice clearing its throat. Shade turned around to see what it was and saw Daxys standing several feet behind him. Daxyz then spoke, "Sorry to interrupt you two but Shade I need to talk to you for a bit." Shade could sense that Daxyz tone was more serious then usual so he knew this was probably a more serious matter. He turned back to Nemi and smiled, "I probably have to do some work for Daxyz. I'll be back a bit later okay?" Nemi then nodded. Daxyz smiled and nodded at Nemi before he turned around and walked down the hall way expecting Shade to follow. Shade and Daxys walked to the front door of the house and put on their shoes before walking out, neither said a single word. Shade could see Nemi peeking at them down the hallway. He then turned to her and smiled as he waved to her before him and Daxyz walked out. As soon as they walked out Daxyz smirked and said "Played it cool back there huh?" Shade chuckled softly, "Yea yea, anyway you seem more serious then usual what's up?" He and Daxyz walked down the empty street in front of the house. It was still very cloudy outside and the pavement was wet from the rain. At least it had stopped raining for a while. After several moments of silence Daxyz spoke, "The Rags and us haven't had to fight in quite some time. We stayed on our parts of town and they stayed on theirs. However, since Nemi's dad got caught and a new leader was selected it seems like they think they are tough guys and they have been walking on our side of town harassing people."

Shade did not respond right away so Daxys continued. "That is something we won't allow to happen. We Golds aren't like most gangs as you know." Shade nodded and then responded, "This world is not a pretty place. Most cops are corrupt and most gangs are paying them off so they can do whatever they want. There is little justice in this world…" Daxys nodded as they kept walking down the street. Daxys then spoke, "Exactly. That is why we Golds exist. If the law is corrupt and won't protect the people then we will. And if others see us as evil so be it." Shade didn't know why Daxyz was bringing all this up at a time like this. Shade already knew that the Golds were not like any other gang. The Golds were sponsored by some unknown billionaire, in the most gang filled towns or the towns where the law was corrupt. A Golds base would be set up in an area to counter rival gangs, using less then legal methods. They are not like any other gang, they do not go on raids or rob the innocent. They make money by either robbing the enemy gangs or receiving financial support from wealthy investors who support their cause. However, since the Golds were still going against the law they were referred to as "evil," but if the government is the one that is doing bad things and the Golds are the one's doing good things how can the Golds be referred to as evil? In Shades opinion good and evil is not something that existed in this world. Everyone does something for a reason, despite the Golds protecting innocent people they still do many things considered as bad such as stealing and getting into fights. As well as the government that runs educational systems, hospitals and police officers do so many good things for everyone yet it still does things like allowing Gangs to do anything they want. That is why this world is just to confusing for something to be referred to as good or evil. There is no good or evil there is merely humanity. Shade then heard Daxyz speak, "Yo Shade?" Shade then blinked realizing his mind had wondered and didn't even notice Daxys talking. Shade then spoke, "Oh yea sorry man my mind wandered a bit." Daxys sighed and spoke, "Yea I figured, sorry for getting all philosophical on you, anyway our job right now is to get a group of Rags off our area." Shade didn't seem to show any emotion as he spoke, "How many?" Daxys then replied "A group of 6. According to my sources they are all pretty buff guys so we have no chance going just the two of us. I called in some others to help us out, hopefully we can just scare them away without the actual need for conflict." Shade nodded. They waited on the side of the road for several minutes until a black van pulled up beside them. The doors to the van swung open and inside were a group of about five males, each armed with some sort of machine gun. Shade and Daxys got in the van and as the door closed Daxys spoke, "So we are going to do this the usual way, everyone clear on the protocol?" The group of deep male voices all responded at the same time. "Yup." Shade nodded as well and sat back on an empty chair in the van relaxing before they got to where they were going. Everyone was mainly quite except for two guys in the back talking about a soccer game they had seen the other day. It was like the calm before the storm. Finally the van came to a stop, Shade opened his eyes to see where they were. There was a group of 6 tall buff men harassing some elders down the street. They seemed to be very busy so they did not even notice the van. Daxys got up and opened the van door getting out, after getting off he then spoke, "Come on Shade." Shade nodded and got out of the van walking beside Daxys. They walked straight up to the 6 Rags members without anyone else beside them. They both seemed perfectly calm however. They walked close to the Rags who all had their backs turned. Daxys spoke in a voice far more fierce then his usual one, "Hey morons, you got five seconds to leave those people alone and get the hell out of here. You hear me?" The Rags seemed to all turn around at the same time, there was nothing but pure anger on their expressions. "What the hell did you just say to me?" growled a Rags member at Daxys. At that moment when they were all distracted the elders they had all been harassing took the chance to walk away. Daxys seemed a bit relieved to see that innocent people would not be brought into this. The Rags noticed the elders getting away as well and were even more enraged, they each pulled out a pistol they had on them and pointed it at Shade and Daxyz. A different Rags member growled, "Do you have any idea who we are you punks? You think you can just walk in and play a hero? This isn't a videogame or something this is real life, but you'll never learn that lesson since we are about to blow your brains out." Daxys and Shade still perfectly calm, Daxys spoke, "Look, I'll give you all one last chance, put down your weapons and take several steps back, do that and I may be kind enough to spare you." The Rags seemed to get even more enraged by hearing the comment, the same one from before growled again and spoke, "That's it, your dead kid!" It seemed as though at that moment when the Rags were about to shoot, another deep male voice called out, "Move even the slightest inch and your dead." The Rags all turned around to see the five other Golds standing right behind them with machine guns and riot shields. Daxyz then chuckled and spoke again, "As I was saying, put your guns on the ground and back away slowly, I really don't want to have to kill six people in one day." The Rags faces were now filled with fear rather then rage, they all slowly bent down and placed their guns on the ground before standing up and taking several steps back. Daxyz then looked at Shade and Shade nodded knowing what he had to do. Shade walked to where all the pistols were laid on the ground and picked them all up before walking back to Daxyz. As he picked them up however he could feel the hateful glares of all the Rags on him. When he stood beside Daxyz once more with all the pistols in his hand Daxyz spoke again, "Alright now if I ever see your ugly faces in my part of town again harassing my people I won't be so kind, now get the hell out of here." When Daxys said that the Rags all turned around and ran away, as they ran a voice could be heard from one of the Rags saying, "You'll pay for that some day punks!" Shade, Daxys, and all the other males in the Golds all stayed completely unemotional until the Rags were completely out of sight, when the Rags could no longer be seen they all burst out laughing. One of the Golds members spoke while laughing, "Did you guys see their faces? Oh gosh that was priceless!" They all laughed and talked about the experience they just had as they all got back into the van. The trip back to Daxyz place was a lot more talkative then before. Everyone was laughing and enjoying each others company, even Daxys seemed to be more upbeat than usual. Shade feeling a bit tired laid back and closed his eyes once more. A big smile was spread across his lips.

CHAPTER

17

As the van drove back to Daxyz house everyone was just talking among themselves. The conversation was no longer about the Rags they had scared off, it had now shifted to talking about girls. Shade did not really feel like taking part in the conversation, however it made him think about Nemi. He didn't know why that conversation made him think of Nemi, it's not like she was his girl friend. He was just helping her out after all. He then started to think about what happened with Bia earlier that morning. Daxys could see that Shade had a lot on his mind, he then nudged Shade slightly. Shade seemed to come out of his deep thoughts and looked at Daxys with a slightly surprised expression. "Good to have you back, what the hell has you so deep in thought man?" Said Daxys in a joking tone. Shade just shook his head and replied, "Don't worry about it man." Daxys did not want to pry to deep if Shade did not want to talk about it so he casually changed the topic. "Hey until this thing with that Nemi chick ends you're going to be staying at my place alright?" Shade nodded and responded, "Yea I was thinking the same thing." Daxys then spoke again, "I'll drop you off at your place. Just pick up some cloths and stuff you need for the next couple days, alright?" Shade nodded, he was thinking of doing that anyway since he had been wearing the same shirt for two days now. The van dropped Shade off at his building and Daxys told Shade to call him if he needed a ride. Shade however said that he will just take a bus not wanting to bother Daxys. Shade stood in front of his building. He remembered how this is where he was put at gun point by two Rags that were after Nemi. He also remembered how he was saved by a sniper. He decided to drop by Albert's place, he had to thank him for having his back twice. Shade went up to his own apartment first and packed up a duffle bag with cloths and whatever else he needed for the next couple days, he then walked out onto his balcony. He looked up at the sky for a moment, it was even more gray then before. Most likely it was going to rain again. He then stood on the ledge of the balcony and threw his duffle bag down into the balcony below. Shade was about to jump down himself when he suddenly heard a loud voice from below saying, "Ouch! What the hell?!" Shade recognised that voice all too well and jumped to the lower balcony. As expected Albert was standing there holding Shade duffle bag and rubbing his head. Albert groaned and spoke in a pissed off tone, "You know it's called a door? Fancy invention you should think about trying it sometime." Shade chuckled at his comment and replied, "Ha ha really? Maybe I'll try it sometime." Albert then rolled his eyes and said in a more relaxed tone, "What do you want this time?" Shade smiled and replied, "Just came to check on you man, you really saved me back there." Albert then smiled and replied, "That's what Bros do for each other man, you don't have to thank me." The two of them talked for a while about pretty much nothing, Shade told Albert to stop by Daxys place and Albert said he would make the time, everything seemed so calm and peaceful, however peace does not last very long. Albert's phone began to ring. Albert got up and walked over to the phone before he answered, "Hello?" Several seconds passed and Albert spoke again, "Oh Daxys what up man? Me and Shade were just talking about you." Several more seconds of silence passed and Albert then spoke again, "Yea man he is right here beside me gimmi a sec." Albert turned to Shade and threw the phone to him, Albert then spoke in a quite serious tone, "It's Daxys, he seems quite serious." Shade caught the phone and put it up to his ear, he could hear Daxys voice speak in a worried tone, "Hey Shade, I got a favor to ask you..."

CHAPTER

18

After speaking with Daxys Shade hung up the phone and tossed it back to Albert, he stood there for several moments looking extremely deep in thought and then without another word dashed out of Albert's apartment. Albert yelled after him, "Hey what the hell is going on?" However by that point Shade had already run off, Albert sighed and decided to call Daxys back and see what happened. Shade ran down the stairs of the building and burst through the front door running at at top speed. He could think of nothing but what Daxys had just told him. He remembered his words so clearly, Daxys had said, "Hey Shade, I got a favor to ask. Bia has been missing all day. I called her cell phone but no answer, she never goes off on her own like that so I'm probably being over protective but I'm really worried, you're at Albert's place right? Her usual hang out place is the park near your place, you know the one you two first met in? Could you please check that place for me? Thanks man." Shade did not tell Daxys but he knew exactly why Bia had gone off on her own. He was an idiot earlier that day, and that must have hurt Bia. He spoke to himself as he ran towards the park, "Damn it I'm so stupid! Why can't woman just say what they mean. Ugh." He could feel a slight drizzle of rain but paid no attention to it. He ran into the park and could now see the swing set in the background, he could also see Bia sitting alone on the swing set. He then stopped running and stood in one place, Bia had not noticed him in the distance but Shade did not call out to her. He just realized he did not even know what he was going to say. He truly loved Bia but not in a romantic way, but he knew now she liked him in a very different way. He stood there and tried to think of what he should say until he saw a group of 6 rugged males walk up to Bia. He squinted to see better and then his heart just froze when he saw that those males were none other than the Rags from earlier. He saw Bia try to back away but the Rags were not letting her leave. Shade took one step back slowly, he knew if he walked in there the Rags would recognise him, and after they recognised him they would surely repay him for taking their weapons earlier. His chest was pounding and he thought to himself that he should just back away and call Daxys. He then remembered the first time he met Bia. Back then when she was getting harassed he ran in there without a second thought. He clenched his teeth and took one step forward. He spoke to himself, "The kid version of me has more balls then the adult version, that's just sad." He smirked and chuckled softly to himself. He then, out of nowhere, sprinted at an incredible speed towards where Bia was. He clenched his fist tightly at his side and screamed out in a voice loud enough that everyone would hear him, "Don't touch her!" Shade at his full speed ran and punched one of the Rags right in the face, his punch was so intense the Rags member he had just punched fell to his knees. The other Rags all turned and faced Shade, but Shade looked right at Bia. Bia's eyes were filled with tears and shock when she saw Shade. Shade smirked and spoke in a gentle tone, "Don't worry, there is no way I'm going to let some thugs touch one of the most important people in my life." When she heard those words Bia's eyes began to tear up even more. Shade was so focused on Bia that he did not notice a Rags member sneak up behind him and kick him in the back knocking him down. Bia screamed when she saw that happen. Shade then got back up to his feet and spit out some blood on the ground beside him, he then spoke in a dark tone, "There is six of you and you still have to sneak up on me? Disgusting." The six Rags members all completely enraged charged at Shade. They had a completely one sided battle, Shade getting the life beat out of him. At least Shade was lucky they had no real weapons with them. After a very long battle Shade was face down on the ground trying to stand back up. It had began raining very hard in the time that they were fighting. The six Rags were all around him breathing heavily. One of the

Rags spoke, "Where the hell is this kid getting the energy to keep going?" Another Rags member spoke in a dark tone but also breathing heavily, "Lets just finish him off and get out of here." The Rags all agreed and were all about to finish Shade off when suddenly a police alarm was heard. "Shit!" Said one of the Rags members. One of the other members raised an eyebrow and spoke, "What's wrong with you? The cops don't touch us, calm down." The first Rags member replied, "Maybe on our side of town but this isn't our side if you forgot." The other Rags member then replied, "Oh crap your right, let's get out of here." The six Rags members all ran away until they could no longer be seen. Bia stood there with tears in her eyes. She dropped to her knees beside Shade and lifted his head letting him rest his head on her lap. She was so emotional her voice was much higher than usual as she spoke, "Idiot! Your such an idiot! You didn't have to do that I would have found a way out!" Shades eyes were closed and his breathing was quite heavy. Bia continued to cry even harder. She waited for Shade to make one of his usual snappy comebacks but Shade did not say a single word. Bia's voice became even more shaky, "You can't die on me Shade! You're an idiot and I really hate you sometimes but... but..." Bia cried even harder as she clenched her eyes shut and shouted, "I love you damn it!" Bia's eyes were clenched closed as she cried even harder. Suddenly she felt a warm hand press against her cheek. Her eyes shot open as she looked down at Shade. His eyes were still closed but a very warm smile was spread across his lips. His warm hand on her cheek gently wiped away one of her tears. Shade spoke very slowly and in a very soft voice, "Hey... Crying doesn't suit you..." When Bia heard this, she actually began to tear up even more. Shade kept his eyes closed still and continued to speak in the same slow and soft tone, "You're the most important girl in my life, to me you're way more important than a girl friend will ever be..." Shade coughed from the pain in mid sentence but then continued, "Sometimes... I worry about you even more then Daxys... That's why... I would never let thugs like those guys lay a hand on you." Bia tried to control her tears and wiped them away, she then spoke gently in a slightly shaky voice, "So you're saying that you only love me as a sister or perhaps more?" Shade said nothing for several moments, his eyes were still closed. Shade then began to speak in a very slow tone, "Bia... To me you will always be... "Shade was about to finish his sentence when suddenly he feels Bia's soft lips pressing against his. He slowly opened his eyes and saw Bia now had her eyes closed as they kissed. Bia pulled back after several moments and looked deeply into Shade's eyes. "Never mind. I want to find out that answer on my own." Bia still had tears in her eyes but she still smiled warmly towards Shade. Shade smiled back, he tried his hardest to keep his eyes open but slowly his thoughts began to fade. The last thing he could remember was the sound of a cars wheels screeching to a stop.

CHAPTER

19

Shade could remember nothing past that point. He then woke up and was laying in the same spot he had passed out in but was now surrounded by a thick fog. He felt no pain from his wounds but did not even realise that. The only thing visible in the dark fog was a slightly dim light in the distance. Shade was not even thinking when he started to walk towards the dim light. He wanted to get out of the fog and thought the light could help him see where he was. He continued walking towards the light and it slowly started to get brighter and brighter. He then noticed that actually there were two lights both in the same direction, one light was brighter but a lot farther, the other was very dim but it was very close by. He walked towards the first one and was able to see that it was nothing more than a lantern hanging on a tree branch. He was intrigued by that lantern so he walked up to it and examined it more closely. He then heard a voice from behind him, "Well hello there, and who might you be?" Shade turned around swiftly in a defensive way without saying anything back. He saw a male figure standing before him. The fog was so thick he could not make out any details of the males face, all he could tell for sure was that the male before him was wearing some type of hat on his head. The male voice spoke again, "Woah there bud I have no troubles with you relax, I'm merely wondering where you were heading," Shade slowly dropped his guard before answering, "I don't know where I am so I was just heading towards that bright light." Shade point to the second very bright light in the background." When hearing this the male chuckled softly and spoke, "Oh my no you do not want to go there." Shade was confused and raised an eyebrow as he replied. "Why? Is there something bad there?" The male then chuckled softly once more as he replied, "No it's not a bad place, it's actually a very nice place, it's where I'm heading now." Shade was now even more confused as he asked, "Well then if it's such a nice place can I go there with you?" The man once again chuckled, Shade was wondering what he found so funny, the male then replied, "Well you are welcome to come with me but I'm afraid if you do the fog is so thick you will no longer be able to find your way back." Shade shrugged and replied, "It's better than walking through this thick fog." The man did not chuckle this time he merely spoke in a very kind tone, "That is true, but the only thing is, there are these two girls looking for you back there, if you come with me to the light I highly doubt you'll see them again." When Shade heard what the man said he blurted out, "Two girls? Who?" The male seemed to think about it for several seconds before replying, "Hmm I don't think I caught their names, my apologies." Shade said nothing for several moments so the man spoke once more, "Look it's your choice bud, you can come with me and get out of the fog or go back and try to find the two girl's that were looking for you back there." The man pointed behind himself as he spoke. The man spoke once more, "What's it gonna be kid?" Shade looked at the male figure once more, he then smiled and chuckled before he spoke, "Nah you can go there on your own old man, I'll go look for those girls you mentioned." The male smirked despite the fact that his expression was not visible through the fog and spoke, "Good choice kid." Shade then smiled and replied, "Anyway thanks for telling me, later man." And after saying that Shade dashed back into the fog away from the very bright light. He ran and ran without stopping even though he started to feel a bit light headed. The next thing Shade knew he was no longer running through fog but laying down on something very soft. His eyes were closed so he saw just darkness, he then opened his eyes and saw a light so bright he had to squint to see. He saw that the light was coming from a light fixture on a ceiling. His memory of what had just happened was extremely blurry now and now he felt a slight migraine. He sat up in his bed while rubbing his head softly. He stopped rubbing his head when he looked in front of him and was a bit shocked to see both Bia and Nemi sitting on chairs beside his bed. Both their heads rested on his bed and they were both fast asleep. Shade's foggy memory made him even more confused. He then felt an arm on his shoulder and swiftly turned his head to see who was touching him. He saw Daxys standing beside him with a hand on his shoulder and Albert standing not far behind him. Daxys smirked and spoke in his usual tone, "Hey hey look who's up, way to scare the crap out of everyone Shade." Shade looked up at Daxys with a puzzled expression, Daxys then continued to speak, "You're lucky Albert called me back to tell me you just ran off on your own like an idiot. When he told me that I got in the van and got there as fast as I could." Shade blinked several times and then rubbed his head again feeling his migraine slowly get less painful as he spoke, "How long have I been out?" Daxys then replied, "About twenty four hours or so." Daxys then pointed to Bia and Nemi before he spoke again, "And those two haven't left your side for a single second." Shade then looked back at Bia and Nemi both asleep while resting their heads on his bed. He then turned his head back towards Daxys and spoke, "Thanks man, I owe you one for helping me out once again." Daxys then shook his head and spoke in a more serious tone, "Shade you singlehandedly saved my little sister from six of the most brutish Rags I've ever seen, if anyone owes anyone I'm the one that owes you." Shade chuckled and replied, "Naw man I didn't..." Before he even finished he was interrupted when he heard Nemi's voice speak, "S...Shade?!" He turned to see Nemi rubbing her eye after she had just woken up. When Nemi said that Bia also slowly got up and yawned slowly before speaking as well, "Shade! Your okay!" Shade looked at the two of them and rubbed the back of his head as he spoke, "Haha yeah I'm okay now..." Before Shade could even finish he was jumped by the two girls, they both wrapped their arms around him and in very high pitch voices they both started to tear up and talk about how worried they were. Albert and Daxys chuckled and walked out of the room deciding to give them some space. That is how another exciting chapter in Shades life slowly draws to a close, however little did Shade know the events he experienced in the last couple days would not even be able to compare with what was to happen now.

CHAPTER

20

That night Daxys and Albert had to come and almost physically drag Bia and Nemi out so that Shade could get some rest. Shade was still very soar and had some very bad bruises but other than that he was alright. After sending the girls to their rooms Daxys walked into Shades room and spoke in a soft tone, "So how are you feeling man?" Shade shrugged before replying, "Eh I'm alright now I guess." Daxys said nothing for several moments before speaking, "Good, Good... Okay look man, I kinda need your help, I would never ask you to help in your condition but I really got nobody else available." Shade raised an eyebrow when he heard what Daxys had just said before he replied, "Wait seriously? Why is everyone so busy? We usually can't find stuff to do around here." Daxys chuckled softly for a moment but then got very serious, "The Rags keep stepping on our territory more and more, the six you met were nothing compared to the groups of ten or twenty that are now crossing over on our territory. All our available men are trying to push them back but I don't know where they are getting so many Rags, it's like they are all fixated on taking over our turf." Shade thought for a moment before looking at Daxys with a very concerned look in his eyes as he spoke, "You think that they are trying that hard to find Nemi?" Daxys said nothing for several seconds and Shade took the silence as a "Yes." Shade then sighed and spoke once more, "So what do you want me to do?" Daxys then spoke in a very gentle tone, "You won't have to do much, Albert has a lead to where the Rags most recent base is and we want to investigate that source. However, the only problem is that the person with the information apparently wants to meet us at a bar somewhere." Shade didn't know what Daxys was getting at when he raised an eyebrow and spoke in a questioning tone, "So?" Daxys then continued to speak, "The bar he wants to meet at is deep inside the Rags turf." Shade seemed very surprised at what Daxys said and then spoke in a very loud tone, "Wait what?! That sounds so much like a trap it's not even funny! Who are we going to meet there anyway?" Daxys sighed and spoke again in a calm tone, "Relax Shade, the man we are meeting is apparently very close with Albert, the cops on our side are looking for him so it's not that he wants us to go there it's more like he can't come here." Shade was still a bit suspicious but kept quiet and let Daxys continue talking. Daxys then spoke again, "Besides even if it is a trap you won't be coming into the bar with us. I merely want you to wait outside and keep watch while me and Albert go in and talk to the guy." Shade seemed almost offended when he heard Daxys say that. "Wait what do you mean keep watch? I can't leave you and Albert by yourselves in a bar that is in the middle of Rags territory." Said Shade with a very concerned tone. Daxys sighed since he knew this would be Shades reaction, Daxys then spoke in a very serious tone, "Look even if you wanted too help, in your condition I wouldn't let you go inside either way. Now I really need you to keep watch for me and Albert tomorrow, can you do that?" After several moments Shade decided to swallow his pride and then simply nodded showing that he will do as Daxys asked. Daxys then smiled and spoke, "Thanks man, I knew you would help me out. Now get some rest, you'll need it for tomorrow." Shade once again simply nodded and watched as Daxys walked out of his room. He laid back and relaxed for an hour or two but he could not fall asleep, he was asleep for a whole day after all. He decided to get up out of his bed and walk to the kitchen to get himself some water. The halls were very dark and he was feeling a bit light headed after being in bed for such a long time. He tried to feel his way around the hall way mainly to see if he could feel a light switch. There was a large window at the end of the hallway but it was very cloudy outside so not even the moon gave any light. It was practically pitch darkness. As he ran his hands along the wall he was moving at a pretty fast speed, he just wanted to find the light switch and turn it on already. However, in the rush, all of a sudden Shade felt another person ram into him in the darkness. Shade still feeling a bit light headed lost his balance and fell backwards. He could also feel the person he had bumped into falling right on top of him as well. It was still completely dark. However now a very sweet female voice was heard speaking, "Ouch, oh gosh I'm so sorry I couldn't find the light switch." Shade groaned slightly in pain after falling hard on his bruises, however afterwards Shade spoke in his usual kind tone, "No no it's my fault, I was looking for the light switch too." The female voice then spoke in a slightly surprised tone, "Wait, Shade? Is that you?" Shade still feeling light headed could not really tell who the voice belonged to. However right at the moment the clouds outside seemed to get less thick and moon light flooded the hall way. Shade was actually quite surprised when he saw Nemi laying on top of him. Shades voice seemed a bit surprised as he spoke, "N..Nemi? Shouldn't you be asleep?" It was still pretty dark but Shade could still notice Nemis face getting crimson red from how hard she was blushing. She quickly got to her feet and turned the other direction feeling embarrassed. Shade then got to his feet as well, he assumed Nemi was up for the same reason he was, he then spoke in his usual kind tone "Hey want to come with me to the kitchen to get some water?" Nemi then turned around to face him, she was still blushing but nodded. They walked to the kitchen together and turned on the lights. Shade got two glasses of water for the both of them. They sat beside each other at the kitchen table. They were sitting very close to each other but nobody said anything for quite some time. However, after a while Nemi broke the silence when she spoke, "The Rags... They are looking for me aren't they? It's the reason this place has become so hectic lately." Shade was a bit shocked to hear her say that and did not respond to her comment in any way. Nemi continued to speak, "I really like all the people I met here, it makes me so sad to think that I'm causing them so much trouble." Shade still said nothing when hearing her say that. Nemi continued to speak, "I keep thinking that they will find me soon." Her voice got a bit shaky, she had a smile spread across her lips but a small tear could be seen in her eyes. She continued speaking, "But you know... I wouldn't feel that bad if they found me. If they take me away at least everyone would get to stop fighting to protect me. Stop risking their lives for me when I haven't even known them that long, maybe it would be better if..." Nemi was interrupted suddenly by Shade, he spoke in a kind yet firm tone, "Hey. I don't want to hear that understood? The Rags and Golds have always been fighting so it's not a surprise they are on our turf. You have no need to worry. They won't be able to find you, and if they do I will tear through an entire army of Rags and bring you back here. I don't care what the odds are, I'm telling you I would bring you back here. I don't care how hard it is or how long it will take, if you are ever taken from me I will bring you back. So just trust me okay? I promise you that everything will work out." Nemi was at a loss for words when hearing him say such words. She blushed even more but was not embarrassed about it this time. She giggled softly before wiping the tear from her eye, she then spoke in a very soft tone, "You won't even let me feel bad for myself will you?" Shade smirked and spoke in a slightly arrogant tone, "Nope." Nemi giggled a bit more when hearing that and then looked at him with a sweet and innocent look in her eyes as she spoke, "I know you've done so much for me but could you do me just one last favor?" Shade wondered what she could possibly want so he smiled warmly and replied, "Sure. What would you like?" Nemi bit her lip slightly for several seconds before she spoke, "Just close your eyes." Shade was a bit confused at first but did as she asked. Before he closed his eyes he saw Nemi blushing more than he ever saw her blush before. He then felt Nemis soft lips pressing against his. For the first time that night Shades cheeks were even redder then Nemis.

CHAPTER

21

Shade woke up the next morning alone in his room. He sat up in his bed as a smirk spread across his lips when he remembered what happened last night. He looked at the clock and it was barely ten a.m. He wanted to go back to sleep however he knew he had to go help Daxys and Albert today. He got dressed quickly and walked out of his room towards the kitchen. He looked out the window for a moment and saw that it was raining outside again. He walked to the kitchen where he saw a male whose name he did not know sitting at the table. Shade thought the male looked familiar so he sat down beside the male at the table. Shade then spoke, "Morning" The male was drinking a cup of coffee as he sat at the table, he turned to Shade and replied, "Hey there, good morning. You're Daxys friend right? Remember me I was in the van when we went to take care of that group of Rags" Shade then remembered why that male had seemed so familiar, he then spoke in an upbeat tone, "Oh right I knew you looked familiar." Shade then put out his hand, "I don't think I caught your name, I'm Shade Hunter," said Shade. The male took Shades hand and shook it as he spoke, "I'm Krayton, kinda new here so yea." Shade and Krayton chatted for a while about pretty much nothing until Daxys walked into the kitchen, he looked at Krayton and spoke in a slightly serious tone, "Aren't you supposed to be out on patrol?" Krayton looked back at Daxys and spoke in a nervous tone, "I've been waiting for the van to pick me up.

I don't know where they are." Daxys was quite for several moments before he spoke in the same serious tone, "Just make sure you're not skipping out on work, we really need help around here for the time being. Shade let's go." Shade then nodded and said good bye to Krayton before following Daxys. They walked outside and stood in front of the house. Daxys mood seemed to get a lot lighter but still quite a bit serious. "That Nemi girl is still asleep in her room, which is kind of odd because she is usually one of the first people to wake up," said Daxys in a dull tone, most likely just making conversation while they waited for their ride. When hearing this Shade could not help but try to change the topic. He spoke calmly as well, "Well Bia is also asleep, they were probably just tired." Daxys seemed to disregard Shades comment, he then spoke in a pretty serious tone, "Hey remember when I asked you to look that Nemi girl over and see if she had anything on her that could be used as a tracker?" Shade seemed slightly surprised at Daxys question but still replied in a calm tone, "Yea man I looked her over, but I don't see the point in it I mean she is wearing Bia's cloths and had no electronics on her when I met her so yea. The only thing she has that we didn't give her is a bracelet she wears on her right hand. However I don't think a bracelet is something we should worry over." Daxys looked at Shade with the same serious expression as he spoke, "Did that bracelet have a pendant by any chance?" Shade thought back for a moment, he then replied, "Yeah actually, it had a lapis stone on it which I think is pretty clever since her last name is Lapis. Why do you ask? Don't tell me you are getting paranoid man." Daxys had a very serious expression now and seemed to be very deep in thought, however after several moments his expression lightened and he smiled towards Shade. "Yeah you're probably right, but just to be safe I'll check out her bracelet when we get back." Said Daxys as he saw a large van turn on their street. They both looked towards the road and saw Albert's van driving towards them. The van came right beside them and the back doors slowly opened. Albert could be seen at the front wheel of the van, he smirked and looked towards Shade and Daxys as he spoke, "Hey there guys, get on I wanna get this over with fast." Shade and Daxys got into the van and after the doors closed the van began to drive. Daxys was in the front seat beside Albert and Shade was in the back seat. Albert spoke in a slightly serious tone now as well, "Hey Daxys, remember we are going into Rags turf, are you sure nobody will recognise you?" Shade didn't like how serious everyone was being but knew it was for a good reason. Daxys replied to Albert in the same serious tone, "I hope not, we won't be there for that long anyway, we get out of the van, go in the bar, talk and get back. Besides most Rags are trying to push onto our turf right now so we should be good." After Daxys said that it got quite for a while, Shade broke the silence when he said, "Hey Albert, how do you know that guy anyway?" Albert was quite for several moments before he spoke in a slightly sad tone, "He... was a really good friend..." Shade could tell that Albert did not really want to talk about it so he didn't keep talking about that. It was a pretty quiet drive until finally they reached the bar they were going to. Shade looked out the window of the van, it was clear that they were in Rags territory now. There was graffiti everywhere and the people seemed nervous to even be walking on these streets. The three of them walked out of the van and before Daxys and Albert walked into the bar Daxys told Shade to wait out there and keep watch. Daxys also gave Shade a cell phone and told him to call Daxys if he saw any Rags or police. On the Rags turf the Rags and police were pretty much the same, the Rags paid off the cops to do pretty much anything the Rags told them too. Daxys and Albert had gone into the bar and Shade was standing outside of the bar on his own. He felt quite bored as he leaned against the wall of the bar. He was lost in his thoughts as he looked up towards the sky. Suddenly he heard an oddly familiar voice speak beside him, it said, "Well well we don't see many new faces around here." He turned around and saw a guy, around his age standing beside him. The male beside him was dressed in ripped jeans, red shoes, and a rather flimsy shirt, he also wore a grey hat. Shade then raised an eyebrow while looking at the male, "Do I know you?" The male then replied, "Naw bro I'm just surprised to see a new face around here, most people try to get away from this place not go to it, you know what I'm saying?" Shade agreed with the male so he nodded and spoke in a calm tone, "Yea I know. Maybe the government should do something about it." The male then chuckled as he spoke, "Well the new mayor said he would change things for the better, and slowly I personally think things are getting slightly better. What was that guy's name, Alex Hunter if I remember correctly." Shades eyes widened in shock but he tried to not physically react to strongly to that statement. He never knew his father, Alex Hunter, moved so high up in the government that he was now a mayor. The other male continued to speak when he saw Shade remain quite. The male said, "Yea, he apparently had a son that ran away about 4 years ago, I remember he gave in a resignation shortly after that." This was the first time Shade had heard about this. He rarely listened to political news since he had hated being a part of it so much at one point when he was younger. Shade then spoke in a rather calm tone, "Hmm yea I think I heard of that guy, there was probably a reason his son ran away. I mean it was clear just by watching the news that he was extremely harsh on his son, I don't blame that kid for running away." The male nodded before replying in the same calm tone, "That is true yes, but that is the reason he resigned didn't you know?" Shade again was shocked to hear this for the first time. The male then continued, "He apparently became much kinder to the younger daughter after the son ran away and after being out of politics for about 3 years he went back in and was recently elected mayor." Shade then thought about his youngest sister, she was the only reason he did not run away until he did. The younger sister always stood up for Shade when the dad was yelling at him, and that made the dad get angry at his sister as well. One of the other reasons he ran away was hoping that if he was no longer around his father would at least be nicer to his sister. Therefor he was extremely happy to hear this. Shade then spoke, "Well it seems everything worked out for the better I guess, as long as that old prick is kinder to his daughter. Hey by the way man I never caught your name." The male then smiled and replied, "Yo man all my buddies just call me Dawg" Shade raised an eyebrow but figured the unusual name was right for this unusual guy. He was about to introduce himself as well when suddenly the door to the bar opened and Daxys and Albert walked out. Albert spoke, "Yo Shade, we are done here, let's go." Shade then turned around to look at Albert and said, "Okay let me just say bye to Dawg." Albert and Daxys both raised an eyebrow as they spoke almost at the same time, "Huh?" Shade turned around and saw that Dawg was no longer standing there, Shade figured that Dawg just had to go so he turned back to his friends and said, "Never mind." The three of them got in the van and started the drive back.

CHAPTER

22

The ride back was not as tense as the ride there. Shade asked, "So did you guys get any good info from that guy?" Albert stayed silent while Daxys answered, "Nope, it was a dead end. The base he knew about was old news. They switched their base at least two times since then." Shade had a slightly disappointed expression as he replied, "Oh... But you guys don't seem very down about not getting any info?" Albert then cut into their chat and spoke, "We got some info about how they are planning to slowly invade our turf to search for Nemi so it's not like we got nothing. Not that we didn't know that but it's still good to confirm." Daxys smirked and spoke in a non serious tone, "Nah Albert is just glad he got to meet up an old friend." Shade chuckled at that comment as Albert rolled his eyes at Daxys comment and spoke, "Ahh shut it." It all seemed very calm and relaxed. However, the calmness was quickly ended as soon as they all got back to Daxyz house. There was horror in the eyes of all three of them as they sat in the van looking at the house in front of them. There were several smashed windows and the front door seemed to have been rammed down. "What... the hell...?" Were the only words that could escape Shades lips. Daxyz burst open the door to the van and quickly ran inside the house. Albert and Shade were not far behind him. The inside of the house was just as bad as the outside, almost everything was smashed and a lot of furniture was knocked over. Shade and Albert did not know where Daxys ran off too as they looked around the house, it was a big mess but nothing seemed to have been stolen at least. Daxys roaring voice was then heard from upstairs, "Where is Bia?!" Shouted Daxys roaring voice from the second floor. When hearing this both Shade and Albert ran upstairs. They could see when reaching the top of the stairs that Daxys was holding Krayton up pressed against a wall. Krayton seemed to be very beat up but the wounds did not look fresh so it was clear Daxys was not the one that caused them. Shade put a hand on Daxys shoulder and Daxys looked Shade in the eyes. He understood Shade wanted him to calm down so Daxys dropped Krayton and angrily went downstairs. Krayton slid against the wall slowly when Daxyz let him go. He then sat back against the wall breathing heavily. Shade went in front of him and got down on one knee. Shade groaned slightly when doing so due to the fact that his own wounds were not yet completely healed. However, he was not thinking about himself in the slightest, he spoke as kindly as he could, "Okay look man, you gotta tell us what happened here." Krayton sat back against the wall breathing heavily as he spoke, "I tried to stop them, there were just to many, I really did try but I just couldn't stop all of them." Shade's tone got more stern as he replied, "Okay look you have to calm down, who is this 'them' you are talking about" Despite the question Shade was pretty much already sure who it was that did this. Krayton then replied, "The Rags..." Shade was not surprised by his answer, he then spoke, "What about Nemi and Bia, what happened to them." Krayton then got silent for several seconds before replying, "There was about three of them dragging Nemi away, I was trying to push several back so there was nothing I could do. Then Bia jumped in and tried to hit one. I didn't really see what happened but they took her away also. Then after beating the crap out of me the only reason they left me alive is to tell Daxyz not to mess with the Rags. That's all I know man I swear." Shade nodded and spoke in a forgiving tone, "That will do, thanks." Shade groaned again while standing as it was also very hard for him to stand up. He turned back and saw Albert standing there looking very deep in thought. Shade then spoke to Albert, "Get this guy into a room and try to patch him up, I'll go down and talk to Daxys" Albert did not reply, he merely nodded in agreement. Shade walked down stairs and saw Daxys was on the phone, all he could hear Daxys say was, "Yea I thought so... Get back as soon as you can, peace." Shade walked beside Daxys as he hung up. Daxys was quite for several minutes as his hand was pressed against his forehead, he clearly seemed to have a very bad migraine but he had no time to deal with that. Daxys turned to Shade and spoke in a very serious tone, "Hey, remember I told you to check out Nemi and see if she had anything that could look like a possible tracker. You never got back to me on that." Shade already knew that Daxys was thinking that the Rags were able to track Nemi. Shade spoke in an also serious tone, "Dude when I looked her over she was wearing Bia's cloths and everything else I assume you already checked out. The only thing she was wearing that didn't belong to Bia is this bracelet she had, but I don't see how..." Shade was interrupted by the sound of Daxys loudly slapping his own forehead. Daxys was covering his face and stayed completely silent for several moments before he started to softly chuckle. That soft chuckle slowly grew into a loud, almost insane, laughter. At that moment the only thoughts that circled his mind were that Albert was busy taking care of the injured, Bia and Nemi were kidnapped by Rags, and Daxys the one guy who could always keep his cool and work things out had apparently gone insane. "Well I'm curious how this one will play out..." Shade thought to himself.

CHAPTER

23

At about the same time as the boys had just found out about what happened there was another story taking place. Nemi and Bia were sitting beside each other in the back of a car. They were both blindfolded and their hands were tied behind their backs. They were both very scared but tried to keep on a very calm expression, they did not want to give the Rags the satisfaction of seeing them afraid. Bia was a bit more used to things like this happening so she tried to calm Nemi down. She was very careful however, she heard the Rags voices coming from the seats in front of them so she assumed they would be too distracted to notice her and Nemi speaking. Bia spoke in an extremely silent voice, "Hey, keep calm okay? We will work something out. We just gotta keep calm right now." Nemi nodded, not thinking that Bia was blindfolded and could not see her nod. Nemi than spoke in an also very silent voice, "Your brother is a gang leader right? He must be used to this stuff and is working out a plan to save us right?" Nemi had a very slight bit of hope in her voice when she said that. Bia did not respond for quite a while. Nemi could then hear Bia speak in a slightly uneasy tone, "Well... Yes my brother is a genius, when the scenario does not have anything to do with me..." Nemi was confused and replied, "What do you mean?" Bia again waited several moments and spoke, "This happened to me twice before. My brother who was always in control panics when the scenario has something to do with me, and when he panics he is pretty much a bigger idiot then Shade." Nemi seemed to be a bit upset when Bia referred to Shade as an idiot, "Hey that's not very nice, Shade is such a kind person, don't call him an idiot." Said Nemi in a slightly stern tone. When hearing this Bia could not help but giggle softly, she tried to keep as silent as possible. Bia laughed not only because she found it funny how protective Nemi got when she mentioned Shade but for another reason as well. Nemi was confused when she heard Bia laugh and got even more agitated. Nemi spoke in the same tone as before, "What's so funny?" Bia giggled a bit more before responding, "No, no, don't get me wrong, when I call him an idiot I do not mean it in a bad way. Shade is an incredibly kind person, the kind of person who..." Bia's tone got a bit more serious, almost a bit sadder in a way, she continued to speak, "The kind of person who always jumps in to help without thinking about what may happen, the type of guy who would get in fights with six of the toughest looking guys without a second thought just to protect the people he holds close. He always smiles and keeps positive despite how bad things get, he never thinks of what happened just how to fix it." Bia's voice got a bit sadder once again, "He is the type that never realises what is going on but would still jump in to help in a heartbeat. And a person like that can only be described as an idiot..." Bia took another short pause before continuing, "I love that idiot." Nemi was at a loss for words when hearing Bia. Nemi always knew that Bia also liked Shade but never imagined it to that point. Nemi smiled slightly when hearing this, speaking about Shade somehow calmed her down, for a brief moment the two of them were not even scared about what would happen. Nemi actually thought that Shade's attitude might be rubbing off on them. However, their calmness did not last long, several moments after Bia had stopped talking they could feel the car come to a very rough stop. They could hear the back doors to the car open. A deep male voice spoke in a very stern tone, "Get up." Bia and Nemi both did as they were told, they could feel the hands of some Rags help them get out of the car. Bia felt disgusted just to feel their hands touching her. They were forced to walk where the Rags led them, neither of them had any idea where they were. They could then hear the sound of a large metal door opening slowly. They were then forced to continue walking forward. After several more steps they were able to hear the same door slam closed behind them. Nemi shivered slightly when hearing the door slam as she was now very afraid. Then they both had their blindfolds removed. They could now see that they were inside a small room filled with many boxes, most likely they were in some kind of storage room. There were five Rags in that room with them, one of the Rags looked at the ugliest Rags member there and spoke in a dark tone, "The boss won't be here for a while so what do we do with them until then." The ugliest Rags member smirked darkly and spoke, "Well first off go and check these young ladies if they have anything valuable on them we can take" The other Rags all smirked when hearing this, a majority of them were all looking at the bracelet on Nemis right arm. The one Shade had also looked at when she snuck into his room the first night she spent at Daxys place. Nemi and Bia still had their hands tied so they could not resist when the Rags started to lay their hands on them. The Rags took Nemi's bracelet first, Nemi tried to stop them but it was in vain. She started to tear up as she spoke in a very sad tone, "Please don't take that, it's the only thing that I have left of my father!" The Rags cared very little for Nemi's cries. The Rags also found that Bia was wearing an also rather nice and expensive looking ankle bracelet on her right ankle. Bia knew that it was useless to argue so she did not say anything as they took her ankle bracelet. They had nothing else of value that the Rags would want so the Rags then backed off. The ugliest Rags member spoke again but not towards the girls. He said, "Well it shouldn't take C to long to get here." The ugliest Rags member turned to one of the other Rags beside him, "You can keep watch over them for now, come on guys lets go." The other Rags left and just the one Rags member remained. He had a gun on him so Nemi and Bia did not even think to try anything. The Rags member sat on a chair beside the main door and started to text on his phone, not saying a single word towards the girls. Nemi and Bia slowly scotched to a back corner of the room where they could quietly talk without being heard. Not that the Rags member would notice either way, he seemed to be very focused on his phone. "Those animals... How dare they touch my bracelet..." Bia seemed extremely angry. Nemi thought her ankle bracelet was important to her just like how her own bracelet was important to herself. "Who did you get that bracelet from?" Said Nemi in a soft tone. Bia replied, "My brother gave it to me a couple years ago on my birthday, its my favorite." Nemi understood why she was so angry,

Nemi was also very sad her bracelet was taken away. It was the only thing she had to remember her father by. Bia sighed deeply and spoke in a soft voice, "Those idiots better come and save us quick..." Bia then shivered slightly before speaking again, "Ugh and to top it off it's so cold in here."

CHAPTER

24

At around the same time as the girls waited for the guys to come rescue them, the guys were having some problems too. Shade stood beside Daxys as Daxys seemed to pretty much be losing his mind worrying about his sister. Shade clenched his fist tightly as he watched Daxys laughing insanely to himself. Then, without a second thought, Shade punched Daxys in his left cheek. Daxys immediately stopped laughing. Daxys slowly pressed his own hand against his own sore cheek, he looked at Shade with an unusually calm expression. He spoke in an unusually calm voice as well, "What the hell was that?" Shade responded in a very hesitant tone, "Well you were panicking, that's what they do in the movies, you are calm now aren't you?" Daxys then realized that Shade was actually right and that he truly had calmed down. Daxys then spoke in a very calm tone, "Well I guess you're right, however don't forget..." Daxys clenched his fist and without any warning in the blink of an eye he punched Shade extremely hard in his right cheek. After punching Shade Daxys continued speaking, "One for one." Shade stumbled several steps back and then spoke in an angry tone, "Agh, what the hell man I just tried to calm you down!" Daxys now seeming to be back to his usual self responded in his regular tone, "Yes and I appreciate it." Shade had his fist clenched and was just about to start a huge fight with Daxys when Albert's voice called from behind them, the voice spoke in a slightly annoyed tone, "Can you two idiots kill each other later? We actually have serious stuff to deal with." Shade unclenched his fist when hearing this, he just thought he would get Daxys back later. Daxys also agreed with Albert and nodded. The three males all stood there, nobody said anything for several moments until Shade broke the silence. "So what are we going to do." Said Shade in a calm tone. Daxys was the most silent as he seemed to be the deepest in thought. Suddenly Daxys seemed to get an idea, he dashed upstairs without saying another word. Shade and Albert both raised an eyebrow wondering where he was going. Daxys walked back down stairs shortly after with a small hand held device with a small screen. Daxys spoke in an optimistic tone, "Alright let's get going." Shade raised an eyebrow a bit confused, "Go where?" He said in a confused tone. "Daxys did not pay much attention to Shades question as he spoke, "Don't worry just come with me and let's go. We don't have time to waste. Daxys took a pistol he had hidden under his shirt and tossed it to Shade. "Keep that on you and come on." Said Daxys as he was already heading for the torn down front door. Albert then spoke in a slightly worried tone, "Someone has to stay back and watch the base in case others return." Daxys was pretty much already out the front door as he called back loud enough for Albert to hear him, "Then you stay back, me and Shade are out." Shade looked at Albert and then back at Daxys, he then nodded to Albert and ran to catch up to Daxys. Daxys got in the driver seat of the van and was glad to see Albert forgot the keys in contact. Shade got in the shotgun seat and without any warning Daxys roughly backed up and made a sharp turn as he started to drive down the street at a speed way higher than the legal limit. Shade noticed Daxys focusing on the device he held in his right hand as he drove with his free hand. Shade could not help but ask Daxys the same question again, "Dude what the hell is that? Don't tell me you put a tracker on Bia." Daxys did not answer but Shade took the silence as a certain "Yes." Shade spoke in an unbelieving tone, "Oh god you put a tracker on your sister, does she even know about it?" Daxys sighed as he continued driving and keeping his eyes on the tracker as he spoke in not a very proud tone, "You remember the ankle bracelet I gave Bia on her sixteenth birthday? Well I hid a tracker inside the pendant. Say what you want about it but it's the only lead we have right now." Shade's face got extremely pale when Daxys said this. Shades voice trembled slightly as he spoke, "You...You put a tracker in her bracelet...?"

Daxys was to focused on the tracker and the road to notice Shades pale expression. Daxys responded, "Yea I hid the tracker inside the pendant on her ankle bracelet, she doesn't even know about it, I mean she would probably never wear it if she knew it was a tracker." Shade remembered the first night that Nemi walked into his room he saw her wearing a bracelet with a pendant but never said anything about it. Shade spoke in a shaky voice, "Nemi... Also wore a bracelet with a pendant on it." When hearing this Daxys slammed on the breaks without any warning and glared at Shade, he spoke in a very angry tone, "What?" Shade responded in a very worried tone, "I remember when you told me to look if she had anything that looked like a tracker on her, she was wearing all Bia's cloths and you said you already looked through her things... The only thing she had that wasn't Bia's was a bracelet with a Lapis pendant. But I didn't know there could be a tracker hidden inside it I swear." Daxys was very angry but used all his strength to calm himself down, he then spoke in a calm tone, "Sigh... Look no matter what or how things happened, they still happened. You can apologise for your screw up by helping me save Bia and that Nemi chick too, alright?" Shade nodded. Daxys then began to drive once again as he spoke in the same calm tone, "Good." They did not speak much after that point since Daxys was far too focused on the tracker. Shade soon saw that they were back in the same filthy Rags turf they were in not long ago. They drove even deeper into the Rags turf then before. It seemed that even the roads were getting empty the nearer they got to the location that the tracker was leading them too. Finally they reached the destination they were being led too. It was a rather ugly looking tiny house, however Daxys was staring at it slightly confused. Daxys spoke in a very suspicious tone as he looked at the house and then back at the tracker, "Something is odd, the tracker says that Bia is not in the house, but several meters behind the house. Which means..." They both saw that there was nothing but plain cement surrounding the house. Daxys then spoke in a very serious tone, "That crappy little house is probably just a diversion, they must have a bigger base hidden underground." Shade simply nodded. They both got out of the car and walked to the front door of the small house. Daxys spoke, "There are probably a lot of guards down there and as soon as we open this door it is impossible to guess what will happen, it's your last chance to turn back, so think abo..." Before Daxys could even finish his sentence Shade had kicked down the front door, the house was completely empty except for a set of stairs leading downwards into pitch black darkness. Daxys blurt out, "Hey what are you doing! Don't just jump into things you idiot there could have been twenty guys with guns on the other side of that door waiting for us to open it!" Shade rubbed his left ear and spoke in his usual calm tone, "Your way to loud man, there weren't any Rags waiting for us because they don't know that we even know where there base is. Ugh and I'm apparently the dumb one, now let's go." Daxys opened his mouth as if to make a clever reply but could think of nothing, so he ended up just saying, "Okay..." They walked down the dark stairs and could see a very dim light at the bottom of the stairs. There was a flimsy wooden door there. Shade pulled out the gun he had and kept a firm grip on it as he opened the door with more caution this time. When the door was opened they could see a long poorly lit hallway that led to other hallways. It looked pretty much like an underground maze. There were also two Rags standing in the hallway talking to each other, both of them were holding machine guns. When the door was opened the two Rags quickly pointed their machine guns at Shade and Daxys. One of them spoke in a loud and stern tone, "Yo who the hell are you two." Daxys knew that the pistols that he and Shade had would be no match for the machine guns that the two Rags held, he did not think this through and really did not see how they could possibly get out of this scenario. Shade then spoke in an unusually calm and laid back tone, "Put your guns down boys, I was part of the gang that was attacking the Golds turf." Shade held a tight grip on his pistol and raised it up, putting it to the back of Daxys head. Shade spoke again in the same tone, "This guy here is the head of the Golds base in the district that we were pushing on, with him captured our victory is assured." The two Rags lowered their machine guns and ran up to Shade and Daxys, they seemed to recognise Daxys all too well. One of the Rags spoke, "Whoa it's actually him!" The second Rags member also recognised Daxys and was amazed that Shade had captured him. Daxys expression was filled with fear, he did not know what was going on, was Shade actually going to sell him out to the Rags. Suddenly as the two Rags were so focused on Daxys Shade silently made his way behind the two Rags without being noticed, the two Rags were talking to each other about what to do with Daxys as they focused their attention on him. Daxys however was looking forward and could see Shade sneak behind them, he then realised that this was all part of Shades plan, Daxys scared expression faded and he chuckled softly as he spoke, "Maybe he really isn't an idiot." The two Rags both raised an eyebrow as they spoke almost at the same time, "What are you talk..." While they were both in mid sentence, Shade fired two shots in the back of each of their heads. Daxys chuckled when seeing this as he spoke, "Haha, you really had me going there for a sec bro." Shade ignored what Daxys said as he spoke, "Who were you calling an idiot?" While speaking Shade put his pistol away and bent down to take one of the Rags machine guns. Daxys chuckle again as he also bent down to get the other machine gun, "Huh? I do not know what you're talking about man." Shade rolled his eyes as the two of them started to walk down the hallway while following the trackers direction. The halls they walked down were pretty tall and had very big air vents going along the ceiling. Shade figured it made sense, since they were underground they needed those big vents to get oxygen in these massive halls. As they walked down the halls suddenly they could hear a loud noise coming from the vents above them, Daxys stopped and looked at Shade as he spoke, "Did you hear that?" The noise coming from the vent then stopped. Shade shrugged his shoulders as he spoke, "Dude look at how big those vents are, they probably got rats and stuff running through them." Daxys listened closely for several seconds but could no longer hear anything so he just shrugged and agreed with Shade. Finally they got to a closed steel door. According to the tracker Bia was behind that door, and if Bia was there Nemi was most likely there too. Shade smirked and looked at Daxys as he spoke in a teasing tone, "Last chance to turn back." Daxys rolled his eyes and spoke in the same tone, "Shut up." Daxys placed his hand on the door handle and slowly opened the door. Daxys expected to see his beloved sister behind that door, he imagined Bia running up to him, wrapping her arms around him and telling him how happy she is too see him. He had a huge smirk on his face when opening the door imagining that Bia would think that he is the coolest older brother ever. The smirk on his face however quickly faded. When the door to the room was completely open Shade and Daxys could see nobody else except for four of the ugliest Rags they had ever seen.

CHAPTER

25

At about the same time as that was happening, Nemi and Bia were thinking of ways to get out of the room they were trapped in. It was hard to think though since it was so freezing cold in the room. Bia looked at the Rags guard and he had a jacket on, which would explain why he was not cold as well. Bia could swear she felt a draft coming from somewhere but she could not tell where since the room had no windows. The draft was also not coming from under the main door, which could only mean the draft was coming from an air vent somewhere. She scanned the entire ceiling quickly but could not see an air vent there, which could only mean the air vent was on a wall somewhere behind all the boxes in that room. Bia was able to figure out where the air vent generally was but the only problem now was the guard, it's not like the guard would just sit back while she searched for the vent, and even if she found it not only would the guard not let them sneak away in it but the size of the vent might not even be big enough for a person to fit through. However it was the only thing she could think of so it was worth a try. The first step to Bia's plan is to get rid of the guard somehow. Bia looked at the guard and saw that he was extremely focused on his phone, however he was not texting or anything, he was merely looking at the screen. She thought that the Rags guard may be watching a video but he had no headphones on and without sound what would be the point of watching. Bia realised she had so many thoughts flowing through her head and giggled softly realising how much she resembles her older brother. Nemi then spoke in a silent tone, "That guy is really focused on his phone." Bia nodded realising Nemi was probably wondering the same thing. Bia however realised she was wrong since Nemi seemed to already know why the Rags guard was staring at his phone. Nemi spoke in a silent tone as to only be heard by Bia, "If I had to guess I'd say that guy just got dumped, it's the only time guys stare hopelessly at their phones for so long." Bia thought about it for a while and agreed that her theory made sense. Bia then got a sinister smirk on her lips, the type of smirk she had every time she messed with Shade. Bia spoke in a calm and silent tone, "Follow my lead." Bia did not wait for a reply, she then scotched closer to the Rags guard, her expression suddenly changed to the expression of an extremely innocent little girl. She spoke in a very soft and sweet tone, "E...excuse me sir, is something wrong? You've been staring at that phone for quite a while." Nemi raised an eyebrow wondering what Bia was doing but decided to just sit back and watch. The guard looked up from his phone for the first time yet, he looked at Bia sitting in front of him. Bia then spoke in the exact same sweet and innocent tone, "I...I'm sorry, you don't have to talk to me... Y... you just seemed so sad." The Rags guard fell for Bia's act hook line and sinker. He sighed and then spoke in a very sad tone, "Why do you care if I look sad?" Bia then replied in a very sweet tone, "Well... you just seemed like you were really sad, and to be honest you did not seem as mean as the other ones." The Rags guard sighed and decided that it couldn't hurt to tell Bia about his trouble, at the very least talking about his problems may make him feel a bit better. He began to speak in the same sad tone, "Well you see..." Bia however interrupted him just as he began to speak. She once again used the same sweet and innocent tone, "Umm I'm sorry to interrupt but could you please remove the rope tying up my hands?" She turned around slightly and wiggled her shoulders showing that her hands were still tied behind her back. She continued speaking in the same sweet tone, "I promise I won't try anything it is just so uncomfortable, besides you have a gun so I couldn't try anything even if I wanted to." The Rags guard sighed and figured she was right and there was nothing she could try while he had his gun. He then got up and walked up to her before untying her hands. He then went and sat back down on his chair as Bia sat on the floor in front of him still. Now that her hands were free she took the chance to stretch right in front of the guard trying to look as cute as possible, she then smiled and giggled cutely as she said, "Alright, carry on with your story" The guard could not help but blush when seeing how adorable she was, he then however remembered why he was sad in the first place and his mood dropped once more as he began to speak, "Today was supposed to be the two year anniversary of my girlfriend and me, I had all this planned out, it was really going to be an incredibly romantic day and all... But then I was told I have to take part in this job, and well you just can't say no to the Rags when they tell you what to do... She didn't understand that however, she thought I was putting the Rags before her and so she sent me a text not long ago saying that things are not working out and well... That's how it ended..." Bia couldn't help but feel a bit sad for the guy, she spoke in the cute and innocent tone, "Couldn't you just say you had other plans? I mean how strict are the Rags around here?" The Rags Guard sighed once again as he spoke, "No... it's not that simple, see if they tell you to do something, you do it, if you don't they not only go after you but your loved ones aswell..." Bia smiled when hearing this. She spoke in an even sweeter tone than usual, mainly because this time she was actually sincere. "Aww that's just so sweet, you were trying to protect people then." Bia stood up slowly as she said that, she walked up to the Rags guard and gently sat on his lap. She spoke again in her kindest tone, "Okay look, as soon as you wake up and finish up here you have to call her." Bia slowly wrapped her arms around the guards neck as she spoke, "You tell her how much you love and how you promise to make this up to her. You then take her on the best date imaginable and thank her for putting up with you being in a gang, alright?" The Rags guard smiled slightly until he realised what she had said at the beginning, "Wait, what do you mean wake up..." Before he could even finish speaking Bia pushed an immense amount of pressure on a very sensitive pressure point on the back of his neck, knocking the Rags guard unconscious in mere moments. The guard was now unconscious in Bia's arms as she laid him back on his chair and got off his lap. She then walked up to Nemi and untied her hands. Nemi was amazed at what Bia had done, she spoke in a very excited tone, "That was amazing! The way you knocked that guy out with just a touch. Where did you learn that?" Bia finished untying Nemis hands and then stood back up as she spoke, "My brother taught me, he

71

said that's what I should do if a guy I don't like is hitting on me." They both giggled at that comment as Nemi stood up and stretched as well. "Well what now." Said Nemi in a calm tone. Bia pointed to all the boxes pressed against the back wall. "We have to move all those boxes" Said Bia in a calm tone. Nemi did not know exactly why but after what she had seen she had complete faith in Bia. When removing the boxes both Nemi's and Bia's faces lit up to see a huge frame leading to an air vent. Nemi now knew why Bia had told her to move those boxes. Bia removed the grates to the vent and then climbed into the vent, she waved at Nemi to follow her but Nemi was already right behind her. The girls slowly crawled through the vent for several minutes, they both shivered from how cold it was but they didn't mind being cold as long as they can get out. They seemed to be in the clear, all they had to do was crawl through the vents a bit more and they would make it out, until suddenly they heard a deep male voice. The male voice seemed to be coming from right under them. It was very hard to hear but it sound as though there were two male voices. They were both very scared and suddenly stopped moving. After a while the two male voices could no longer be heard, however even though they could not hear them Bia thought it would not be safe to move yet. So they waited in the freezing cold vent for several minutes. However even after several minutes no other voices could be heard, so they decided it was safe to keep going. At one point the vent started to take a steep upward slope, it was harder to crawl through but they were still able too. Bia was wondering how much further they would have to crawl through these freezing cold vents until they can get out. Finally a light could be seen at the end of the vent. When seeing this they were both inspired so they started to crawl through the vent even faster. Finally when they got to the end of the vent they could see the outside through the vent grates. Bia pushed the vent grate out and they both got out. As soon as they got out they looked back at the very small house the vent was connected too. "Hmm that's strange, how could that house be so tiny? I swear we were crawling through those vents for so long." Said Bia in a curious tone. They then walked to the front of the house and saw the front door wide open. Bia also noticed the stairs leading down so she now knew that the Rags base was actually underground. The two girls did not want anyone else to see them so they quickly started heading down an empty road. They found it strange that the road was so empty. It must be a thing about gang bases. This was Rags turf so neither of them knew it very well. This was one of the smaller Rags bases that not even Nemi knew about. Suddenly they saw a male standing at the side of the road. He did not seem like a Rags member so they decided to go and ask him for directions. As they got closer the male seemed to be around their age. They also both noticed that the male was wearing a hat that seemed kind of peculiar but they did not pay much attention to it. Bia being the more talkative spoke first, "Umm hello, excuse me sir." The male turned to face them and had a huge smile on his face as he spoke, "Why hello there, and who might you two be? Haven't seen you two around these parts before, gosh I'm seeing so many new faces lately." The girls thought that the male was a bit odd but didn't say anything about it. Bia then responded to his question, "My name is Alexis and this is Amy. We are kinda lost around here so we were wondering if you could point us in the direction of a nearby bus station or somewhere we could find a cab." Bia clearly was too careful to give out their real names. The male once again smiled as he spoke, "Well nice to meet you both, they call me Dawg around these parts. Anyway if you want to take a cab just keep heading down this road until you come to the first busy intersection and walk left for about two minutes, there are usually cabs waiting for passengers there. Oh and don't worry about money you can just tell them you'll pay them when they drop you off." Bia raised an eyebrow and spoke, "How did you know we had no money?" Dawg just smiled as he replied in his usual kind tone, "Lucky guess." Bia decided to just drop anything else and thank the man for the information before they got on their way. After thanking Dawg the two girls started to walk down the street until Bia suddenly blurted out, "Oh wait, I actually wanted to ask him where we are right now. It may be useful to tell Daxys where this base is located." Bia quickly turned around as she spoke, "Oh one last question if you don't mind..." Bia stopped herself mid sentence as she noticed that Dawg was no longer behind them. She raised an eyebrow again, "Wait but he was just there?" Nemi tugged gently on Bia's sleeve as she spoke in a very tired tone, "It's okay, he told us where to go let's just go home." Bia nodded and agreed. They both smiled and headed down the road together.

CHAPTER

26

The girls seemed to be in the clear however the guys did not seem to be so lucky. Shade and Daxys could not understand what was going on. They expected to be reunited with Nemi and Bia but were now face to face with four of the toughest looking Rags they had yet seen. The Rags all pulled out pistols in a flash and pointed their guns at Shade and Daxys. Daxys stared at Rags and spoke in a very silent tone, "So Shade, got any plans this time?" Shade did not reply as one of the ugliest Rags spoke over Daxys in a very loud voice, "What the hell? Who are you two clowns?" Neither of them responded since neither of them could think of something to say. The Ugliest Rags member looked at the two of them and chuckled as he spoke, "Ha you think you can just walk in on my turf and act all tough? Maybe if you had a bit more people on your side but we out number you two to one, now drop your guns." Daxys realised that the Rags member was right and dropped his gun as the Rags member said, Daxys thought that he could try to talk his way out of it somehow if he did what the Rags told him. Shade however did not drop his machine gun, he kept a very firm grip on it as a smirk spread across his lips. The ugliest Rags member seemed to get even madder when seeing this as he spoke in a very angry tone, "Hey punk, didn't you hear me? Your buddy already dropped his so no matter what hero move you try out you can't..." Shade did not let the ugliest Rags member even finish what he was saying as he spoke over him in a completely emotionless tone, "Well I guess I should thank you, by acting all tough you pretty much showed me who is in charge here." When hearing this the ugliest Rags member seemed to get even more furious as he spoke, "And what's your point punk? Now drop your gun before we shoot you and your buddy there. He already dropped his gun, you can't possibly shoot four people before we shoot you..." Shade cut into the ugliest Rags speech once again, he spoke in the same emotionless tone, "Your just making yourself look dumber the more you talk. Your clearly going to shoot as soon as I drop my gun. However you know if both sides shoot there would be a fifty percent chance you would get shoot, well now that my dumbass friend here dropped his gun there would only be a twenty five percent chance that you would get shoot. However, since you were trying so hard to make me drop my gun as well it's clear you did not even want to take the twenty five percent chance. Well let me take out the guess work for you." Shade then pointed his gun directly at the ugliest Rags member, not paying attention to any of the other Rags members even a little bit. The ugliest Rags member seemed to actually be a bit scared but did not back down yet, he stuttered slightly as he spoke, "D... don't be a dumb ass, even if you shoot me you will get shoot right back, you're willing to die just like that?" A small smile spread across Shades lips as he spoke in the same emotionless tone, "My life really isn't that important, heck I can't even protect two girls that like me, is there really a point in going on if I can't even do that. The days go by pointlessly, I put on a fake smile and go through my daily routine. If I really were to get shoot down here I honestly wouldn't mind, at least I can take your ugly ass with me as I go." The ugliest Rags members face seemed to twitch slightly when hearing Shades words. Him and Shade stared into each other's eyes intensely for several moments until finally he succumbed to Shades words and lowered his gun, he then gestured with his free hand to the other Rags to also lower their guns. The other Rags members were amazed at how Shade was able to make their feared boss call off a hit. Shade then nudged Daxys with his elbow to bend down and pick up his gun. Daxys was also speechless and amazed at what Shade had pulled off. Daxys quickly bent down and picked his gun back up. The ugliest Rags member then looked at Shade again with pure hatred in his eyes as he spoke, "There, now get the hell out of my base." Shade smirked again and spoke, "No I'm afraid there is one last thing." Daxys thought Shade was insane, how far did he think he think he could go. The Rags leader growled and raised his gun pointing it at Shade once again, the leader of the group growled and spoke in and enraged and hateful tone, "Your really pushing it kid!" Shade smirked and spoke in the same tone, "Now now calm down, think for a second, I'm holding a machine gun at an incredibly close range, with two machine gun it's actually possible that all four of you could die if we spray the bullets." The ugliest Rags members right eye began to twitch with anger as he spoke slowly, not lowering the gun, "What the hell do you want...?" Shade then pointed at the table that all four of the Rags members were sitting at before he spoke, "I want those bracelets." Daxys rose an eyebrow when hearing this wondering what Shade was talking about. He looked where Shade was pointing and his eyes widened to see two bracelets laying on the table that the Rags were sitting around. He recognised that one of those bracelets was the one that he had given to Bia. He assumed the other belonged to Nemi. It made sense now, that is how him and Shade burst into the wrong room, the Rags stole anything valuable Bia and Nemi had on them. Which means that they did not know that either bracelet had a tracker. The ugliest Rags member growled silently as he turned to one of the other Rags members and told him to give those bracelets to Shade. The Rags member nodded and picked up the bracelets off the table. He then handed the bracelets to Shade, Shade took the bracelet but still kept one hand on the guns hilt, not for a moment lifting his finger from the trigger. With his free hand Shade took the bracelets and put them in his pocket. He then without another word began to back away slowly, he nodded at Daxys to signal him that they should back away now. Shade did not break eye contact with the ugliest Rags member for even a moment. As soon as Shade and Daxys were on the other side of the wide open door Shade looked into the ugliest Rags members eyes one last time. A small smirk spread across his lips before he grabbed the handle of the door without any warning and slammed the door closed. As soon as the door was slammed closed he pointed his gun at the door handle and fired a barrage of bullets. "That ought to buy us some time, they would have to smash the door down before they even try to go after us." Said Shade in the same tone that he had used until now. Daxys simply nodded at what Shade said. Shade then spoke again, "Now let's get out of here before they break the door down,

I highly doubt what I pulled off will work again." Daxys nodded again and they both began to run down the long hallways. They turned left on another hallway as they ran. Daxys noticed that Shade was heading to the exit of the underground base. Daxys then spoke in a slightly worried tone, "Wait what about my sister? We can't leave..." Daxys was interrupted by the sound of a door being smashed open and crashing loudly on the floor. The loud sound of the door crashing on the floor was then followed by the sound of many bullets being fired. Daxys shivered just thinking what would have happened if they did not just turn to run down a different hallway. As they ran down the hallway towards the stairs leading upwards Shade replied, "We don't have much of a choice right now, our plan failed the best thing to do now would be to head back and think of a new plan, that is if we can even make it out of here." Daxys did not want to admit it but knew Shade had a point. They could hear the sound of the Rags running down the hallway about to turn on the hallway they were on. They could see the two unconscious Rags that Shade had shot earlier, the door leading upwards was not far. Shade and Daxys smashed through the door and began to run up the stairs, they could once again hear a barrage of bullets being shoot on the hall way they were just on. The Rags must have fired without looking hoping to hit Shade or Daxys as soon as they turned the corner. Shade could not help but feel a bit bad for the two Rags he shot, however there was no time for that. They quickly ran up the stairs and outside of the small house. They stood outside for several seconds thinking about what they should do. They had to think about what to do quickly. Shade then noticed that at the side of the tiny house there was an air vent grate on the floor, this gave him an idea. "Quick, I have an idea." Shade ran to where the air vent grate was, got down on his hands and knees and started to crawl into the vent. Daxys was a bit confused but knew slightly what Shade was planning. He decided that Shade had gotten them this far so he quickly followed him. When they were both in the vent Daxys, being closer to the outside, took the air vent grate and put it back in its proper place. Several seconds past, but those seconds felt like hours. Then the loud sound of the four Rags stomping around outside could be heard. Daxys could slightly hear the Rags voices, he heard them say "They could not have gotten far, get in the car and let's look for those punks!" He then heard another voice, "Hey that van doesn't look familiar" Daxys knew that they had seen his van that him and Shade had drove there in. Another Rags voice could be heard, "If their van is still here they must not have gotten far on foot, quick let's look for them!" Some smashing could be heard and the sound of their voices got more and more silent. Their car was probably destroyed. The voices soon could no longer be heard. Daxys could hear Shade behind him starting to walk down the vent. Daxys then spoke in a very serious tone, "Where are you going?" Shade replied, "To look for Bia and Nemi of course."

CHAPTER

27

Nemi and Bia were still walking down the empty road. They both could not wait until they got to a main road that was not as deserted as this one. For some reason the sheer fact that this road was so isolated and empty made both of them feel uneasy. There were many trees on either side of the road. Trees so thick that you could not even see what was on either side, it felt like they were walking down a hall way with only one possible direction to go. Nemi and Bia both felt very relieved when they finally got to the main road. There were cars rushing in both directions. They both smiled and giggled happily when seeing that they were now on a main road. They felt so happy that they actually turned to face one another and gave each other a great big hug. However, their moods quickly dropped. As they embraced each other they were able to see out of the corner of their eyes that a big gray public bus just passed by them. They stared into each other's eyes for a brief moments before they let go of each other and started to run as fast as they possibly could after the bus. They waved their arms trying to get the attention of the bus driver but they had no luck. They stopped running when they realised that the bus was far too fast to catch and that the bus driver clearly was not going to stop for them. The girls were both breathing heavily. Bia got a bit frustrated and kicked the ground angrily before taking a deep breath. Bia then calmed down a bit and spoke in a calm yet tired tone, "It's okay, don't worry, that guy we met said there should be cabs around here anyway." Nemi was also tired from chasing the bus and as she breathed slightly heavily she merely nodded at Bias comment. They both looked around for several moments before Nemi spoke in a more cheerful tone, "Look there!" She pointed in the direction of the road that had lead them to the main road, several hundred meters behind that road was a big yellow sign that read "Taxi Cab Company" Bia smiled when seeing that and they both started to walk towards it, however they felt a bit uneasy as they walked to the intersection of the road they were first on. The main road seemed to have gotten a bit less busy, it wasn't very busy at first however now there were only one or two cars passing by every twenty seconds or so. As they reached the intersection of the road that they originally walked on just as they were about to cross Bia put out her arm in front of Nemi not letting her cross. Nemi was a bit confused, she was about to speak and ask her what was wrong but before Nemi could even say a single word Bia shushed her. It was extremely quiet for several seconds until the sound of a car motor could be heard. However, there were no cars driving on either side of the main road. There were many trees on the road they originally walked on. They could not see if there was a car coming down that road however that could be the only source of the noise. Fear filled both their hearts. Bia thought that the Rags must have noticed their escape and were now looking for them. Bia grabbed Nemis hand and pulled her into the thick group of trees. When they walked down that road they could not see on either side due to all the trees so Bia hoped that the Rags would not be able to see them either. They both ran behind one of the thickest tree trunks and pressed their backs against it. They both listed carefully and could hear the engine of the car getting nearer. Nemi felt very frightened, they had made it so far it would be so terrible if they got caught again after all the work they put into escaping. The car engine suddenly got a lot more silent which meant it was stopped at the intersection waiting to turn. Bia was also very frightened but decided she had to check who it was. She very cautiously peeked from behind the tree. She could see a rather old black van. She squinted her eyes and was able to recognise the driver as one of the Rags from before. The back seat windows were tinted so she could not see if there was anyone else in the van. The van then turned and started to drive down the road, the car drove slower than the speed limit, Bia figured it was because the driver was looking for her and Nemi. They were very lucky to have that thick grove of trees to hide in, or else who knows what might have happened. Bia then whispered quietly in a slightly rushed and stressed tone, "Alright we should try and get to that cab place quick, I just want to get out of here." Bia turned to get out of the grove of trees until Nemi grabbed her hand not letting her leave. Bia raised an eyebrow as she spoke, "What is it?" Nemi looked down as she held onto Bias arm before she spoke, "Just wait a bit." Bia raised her eyebrow again, "What do you mean wait? Let's get out of he..." This time it was Nemi that shushed Bia. Bia did not understand but decided to trust Nemi and waited. Several seconds passed and surely enough the sound of another engine could be heard in the distance. Bia had no idea how Nemi knew there would be a second car but was very happy she trusted Nemi. If they would have walked out of the grove of trees they may have been spotted before they could run back in. "How did you know a second car would come?" Nemi merely shrugged as she replied, "There were two ways down the road to go, I figured they wouldn't check only one of them." Bia opened her mouth as if to reply but could think of nothing to say. She was a bit embarrassed she did not think of that first but decided this was not the time to worry over things like that. After waiting several more seconds just in case the girls both cautiously got out of the grove of trees. They then wasted no time and jogged up the street to the taxi cab sign, and surely enough right under the sign there was a taxi cab dispatcher building. They walked into the building and saw that inside it was mainly empty. There was a small desk in the back corner of the room they were in. An old man sat behind it. The old man had white hair and a very friendly smile on his face. The girls walked up to him before Bia spoke, "Hello sir, umm we have no money on us but we could pay when we get dropped off if that is okay. We would really like to get out of here as soon as possible." The old man smiled and replied in a very kind yet slow tone, "of course of course. I will call a cab for you two now, where are you heading?" Bia then told the man the address. The man smiled once more and called one of his cab drivers to come pick them up. They had to wait for about five minutes and it was pretty much silent the whole time. After the day that Nemi and Bia went through chatting was the last thing on their minds. Finally Nemi broke the awkward silence as she turned and began talking to Bia, "Do you think if we couldn't find our way out the boys would have come for us?" Bia raised an eyebrow when hearing this, "Psh, those idiots? Yea right." Nemi seemed a bit disappointed when hearing this. Nemi then nodded and replied, "Oh... okay..." Nemi was interrupted by the old man speaking over her. The old man spoke in his same slow kind tone, "The cab is outside waiting for you two." The girls both smiled when hearing this. They thanked the old man and walked outside before getting into the cab. They both got into the back seat and told the driver where to drive them. Bia laid back and fell asleep almost instantly. Nemi giggled from seeing this, realizing she must have been very tired. Nemi looked out the window as the cab drove, she wondered about what she asked Bia before. She was curious what would have happened if they didn't escape, if Shade would have really come to save her. The cab passed by the intersection that leads upwards to the Rags base. Nemi wanted to look up that road one more time as they passed it. That is when she saw something that brought a great big smile across her lips. The cab drove by fast so she wasn't really sure if she saw what she thought she saw. She thought she could possibly just be tired and imagining things, however it was enough to make her smile.

CHAPTER

28

At around the same time as those events were happening the boys were crawling through the vents of the underground Rags base. Neither of them spoke much as they crawled through the vents until finally Daxys broke the uncomfortable silence. He wanted to ask about what Shade had pulled off back there. Daxys remembered Shade saying it was just a plan but for some reason did not fully believe him. Daxys spoke in a very soft and silent tone, "Hey..." Shade was quiet for several moments before responding in the same silent tone, "Yea?" Daxys hesitated for several moments before speaking again, "That whole act you pulled back there, it really didn't seem like you." Shade again was silent for several moments before responding, "Oh yea..? What exactly didn't seem like me?" Daxys had to think about Shades question for a while before responding. "You just... seemed darker in a way, not like the type of person you usually act like." Said Daxys in the same silent tone. Shade chuckled for a brief moment before responding in the same tone, "There are times to smile, and times not too." Daxys agreed with what Shade said but noticed that Shade was trying to avoid his original question. Daxys wanted to ask Shade another question however just as he was about to speak Shade spoke over him in a slightly excited tone, "Hey look up ahead, the grates are missing from one of the vents" Daxys was no longer focused on the question he wanted to ask as he looked past Shade to see what he was talking about. Daxys was also slightly surprised to see the grates from a vent missing. Daxys spoke silently, "Wait, the only reason that vent grates would be missing would be that someone removed them." The boys crawled to the vent with the missing grates and got out. After getting out of the vents they noticed that the vent grates were laying on the floor, this made Daxys cretin that someone must have had removed them. They then looked around the room and noticed that there was a male sleeping while sitting on a chair near the door. Daxys was about to try and think their next move over however Shade was not in the mood to wait. Shade walked to the sleeping male, grabbed him by the collar and shook him harshly while speaking in a deep and rough tone, "Hey, get up, I need you to answer some questions." The male was slowly gaining consciousness but Shade really was not in the mood to wait. Shade then let go of the male and took several steps back before pointing his machine gun at the male. The male's eyes opened slowly, the last thing he remembered was one of the girls he was supposed to watch over climbing on his lap. The male jumped to his feet however when he noticed Shade standing in front of him pointing a gun. Shade spoke in a very rough tone, "You, do you know anything about two girls around eighteen years old, that you damn Rags kidnapped." The Rags member put his hands up into the air to show Shade that he would not resist. The Rags member was very frightened as he responded to Shades question in a frightened tone, "I... I don't know, I was watching over them but then I just wake up with you pointing a gun at me!" Shade was confused for a second, if the Rags member in charge of watching over them did not know where they were it made no sense. Shade then remembered how the grates of the vent in this room were not in their proper place. His face then went blank when he finally realised what had happened. He turned to look at Daxys who must have also figured out the same thing as Shade since he placed a palm over his own face and chuckled silently to himself. Shade lowered the gun and sighed deeply as he looked at the Rags member and then chuckled softly as well. The Rags member was very confused, however Shade lifted the gun once more. Shade spoke again in his deepest tone, "Those girls, why did you kidnap them? And why did you steal this bracelet." Shade pulled out Nemis bracelet and showed it to the Rags member. The Rags member spoke again in the same frightened tone as before, "I don't know, the orders came from higher up, I just did what I was told to do. And I don't know how you got that bracelet but it looks like the one the boss told us to take from the girls. We weren't ordered to take their valuables from higher up, the boss of our group is just greedy." Shade and Daxys could finally put all the pieces together, what made no sense at first now became very clear. Shade then took a step closer to the Rags member as he spoke in a very calm and slightly amused tone, "Hey Daxys, it's funny isn't it? In the time it took us to save them they were already long gone." Daxys chuckled when hearing this and nodded as he responded, "And we call ourselves men..." The Rags member was very confused however that did not matter much. Before the Rags member even knew what was going on Shade used the hilt of his gun to roughly hit the Rags member in the head, knocking him out once more. Shade then sighed deeply and spoke in a slightly sad tone, "Sigh... Well let's go back... The girls are probably already home..." Daxys nodded as they made their way through the vents once more. They exited the vent through the same place that they entered. When they crawled out of the vent they quickly looked around for any Rags members but luckily none were around. They quickly went to check on their car but it was obviously wrecked by the Rags. Shade and Daxys sighed almost at the same time as they began to make their way down the road to the main intersection. Luckily they knew about the main road due to the fact that they drove there. It was a pretty quiet walk, since both males had their pride crushed so severely, they really did not feel like talking. The main road was now visible, however Shade and Daxys still did not know how to get back to Daxys house. Then Shades face lit up all of a sudden. Daxys was looking down at his feet as he walked so he did not notice but what Shade saw was enough to make him cheerful. Shade spoke in a very excited tone, "Dude! You won't guess what I just saw!" Daxys raised an eyebrow as he looked up at Shade. Shade then spoke again in the same excited tone, "I just saw a cab pass by on the main road, maybe there is a cab place nearby!" Daxys then sighed and responded in a very tired tone, "Damn Shade you sounded so excited I thought you saw the girls or the Rags, not a dumb cab passing by on the road..." Shade got a bit mad when hearing Daxys as he responded, "Hey at least we can get home more easily, and if there is a nearby cab place the girls probably found it too, no reason to get all agitated." Daxys then sighed and apologised, he was just very tired from the long day that they had gone through. They walked until they reached the intersection to the main road and surely enough saw the cab dispatching station. Seeing the cab station lifted their spirits slightly but not too much. They walked into the cab dispatching station and walked up to the old man. Daxys told the old man where they needed to be dropped off. When hearing the address that Daxys told him the old man chuckled slightly and then spoke in a very soft tone, "Oh and where are you boys heading? You know I just dispatched a cab with two extremely cute girls heading in the same direction." When hearing that Shade and Daxys both got very excited, Shade spoke in a slightly more excited tone, "Wait, really? What do you mean by 'same direction'?" The old man thought for several moments before responding, "Oh well the place they wanted to be dropped off at was just about ten blocks away from where you want to be dropped off." Daxys and Shade were both a bit confused when they heard the old man say that the girls asked to be dropped off several blocks away from where they were going. Maybe it was just a major coincidence and two girls just so happened to be heading in that direction. But then where were Bia and Nemi? After what the Rags guard said they were sure that Bia and Nemi had snuck out through the vents, there was no other possible explanation. Their cab then arrived and they both got in the cab thinking about what the old man said. It was pretty silent until Daxys broke the silence. Daxys spoke in a stern yet calm tone, "It just makes no sense, the two girls the old man talked about must have been Bia and Nemi, there is just no other possible option." Shade nodded and responded, "But why would they tell the cab driver a different address?" Daxys then burst out in a slightly confused tone, "That's what I'm thinking! Something just doesn't add up!" Shade then thought for a moment but could still come up with nothing. Shade then spoke in a very calm tone, "Dude, I'm sure we are just missing something, there has to be a reason." Daxys then shrugged and responded blunty, most likely from tiredness. "Dude, girls are just stupid, maybe they gave the wrong address somehow." Shade shrugged and agreed as he replied, "Let's just hope that it actually was them and we will see them when we get back home." Daxys nodded. After the long trip back to Daxys house the boys now felt very tired. They paid the driver and slowly walked into Daxys house. They noticed that the house was still slightly wrecked but it was in much better shape. Albert must have worked hard to fix it. When they walked in they were greeted by Albert. Shade and Daxys however despite Albert's greeting looked around franticly. Albert raised an eyebrow as he spoke, "What are you two looking for? And where are the girls?" Shade and Daxys both looked very worried and just as they were about to explain everything to Albert they could hear a knock on the still rammed down door. All three of their heads turned to look at the front door to see none other than Bia and Nemi standing before them. Nemi had a cute and warm smile on her face however Bia seemed to be very angry. Daxys and Shade both were a bit worried when they saw Bia's expression. Bia growled slightly and walked up to Shade and Daxys as she spoke in a very stern tone, "And where the hell have you two been!" Shade opened his mouth as if about to speak, however he was quickly interrupted by Bia who continued to speak in the same tone, "No I don't even want to hear it! We were actually kidnapped in case you haven't noticed, thanks for the help by the way. Oh and why the hell did I see a cab going down the road as we got close to the house? Are you two that dumb? This is supposed to be a secret base, you're not supposed to give your real address! Gosh at least me and Nemi had enough brain to give the cab driver an address 10 blocks away and walk to our 'secret base'! Like honestly if you just give away our real address so easily it's no wonder we got jumped! Ugh men are just so stupid!" Bia through her arms into the air and walked past Shade and Daxys most likely going to rest in her room. Daxys and Shade were completely speechless. Nemi then giggled and spoke in a very cute tone, "Don't worry guys, she is just tired, she is actually very happy to see you." Nemi then giggled before she continued speaking, "Anyway I am also very tired, I'm going to go to sleep as well." Nemi smiled and walked past Shade and Daxys. The two boys merely stood there, both feeling so incredibly stupid. Albert tried his best to hold it in but when he heard the door to the girls room close, he burst out laughing. Albert was laughing so hard he could not even stand anymore and had to sit down. After listening to Albert for several moments Shade then turned his head to face Daxys as he spoke in his usual tone, "So.. umm… its all good?" Daxys blinked several times before responding, "I'm going to sleep." Shade chuckled softly as he spoke in a very tired tone, "I'm getting a drink…" Daxys nodded and chuckled before replying. "Eh your plan sounds better." And so ended another chapter in their adventure.

CHAPTER

29

Shade quickly sat up in his bed. Breathing heavily, he remembered how he had fallen asleep after drinking with Albert and Daxys the night before. He could not remember his dream but knew for sure it was a nightmare. However, Shade knew there were still things he had to get done, so he decided to ignore the nightmare and just blame the alcohol. His head hurt slightly but he was still able to remember the talk he had with Daxys last night before he went to sleep. It was late, and both the girls, as well as Albert, had already fallen asleep. Shade usual expression slowly changed to one of slight sorrow. Despite having a decent amount to drink that night Shade was still able to remember everything him and Daxys talked about.

It was very late at night and Albert was already snoring on a couch in the living room. After having had calmed down a bit, Bia, along with Nemi, had gone and talked to the boys about the adventures they had that day. After the girls finished the boys then told them about the adventures they had trying to rescue them. Despite all that happened, at the end of the day they were all able to laugh over the events that just took place. Thinking back on the events that had taken place Shade was actually glad that everyone was able to laugh. Nemi however did not seem to be as happy as the others. Shade just assumed she was not as use to the drama that happened as the rest of the Golds were. Or at least that's what he thought. The girls got tired at around mid night. That's when Daxys suggested to

Shade that they go up on the roof. Shade agreed and quietly as to not wake the others him and Daxys made their way to the roof. It was very cloudy outside but at the time it was not raining so it was alright. That's when Daxys began to talk to Shade about what the next step for them is going to be. "She can't stay with us. You know that right?" Shade was stunned to hear Daxys say that but did not find his words to be unexpected. Shades tone got a bit aggravated when hearing Daxys say that. "So what are you suggesting? That we just leave her on her own?" Daxys shook his head slowly as he replied in a very honest tone, "No that would be impossible, if I wanted to do that not only would you never let me forget it but now Bia has gotten quite close to that girl as well." A soft smile spread across Shades lips as he heard that. Shades tone went back to normal as he chuckled softly and replied, "So what are you suggesting then?" Daxys was silent for several moments before he replied. "The main Golds base in the North." Shade seemed a bit shock when he heard that, his tone got slightly agitated once more as he spoke, "Wait the far north one? Why that far? That's pretty much like making her leave!" Daxys sighed since he had already known how Shade would react. He then spoke again in his usual calm tone, "Don't start this Shade, you know that I'm sending her to the biggest Golds base in existence. There is no Rags member anywhere who would even think about setting foot close to that area." Shade knew that Daxys was right but for some reason he just did not want to accept what he was hearing. Shades tone seemed more sad rather than angry now as he replied once more, "Do the girls know about your plan?" Daxys nodded slowly before speaking in the same calm tone, "Of course. I talked to Bia myself and then we both talked to Nemi about it. However, Bia even though she seemed really sad while talking, said that if you find out about what's happening you would react like this. That's why Nemi was so quiet earlier and why I brought you up here to tell you what is happening." Shade was speechless, he really did not know what else to say. Shade simply nodded slowly and stood up straight on the roof. He spoke in a very silent tone, "If that is what everyone thinks is for the best then despite what I think you should carry on with that plan. Now if you don't mind I'm heading off to sleep." Shade then left the rooftop without another word. Daxys was actually surprised that Shade didn't put up more of a fight but he knew that deep down Shade understood this was the best possible plan. However, it was obvious to Daxys how sad Shade was as he left. Daxys still not feeling tired decided to stay on the roof for a while longer. He kept thinking about how Shade reacted almost exactly the way Bia had said he would react. "That idiot, I think pretty much everyone knows how he feels except for him." mumbled Daxys silently to himself.

CHAPTER

30

Shade was still thinking very intensely about the night before as he walked out of his room. He was so focused on his own thoughts that he did not notice a person on the other side of his door as he left the room. He jumped back slightly just as he was about to collide with the other person. He then saw Nemi standing before him. She seemed to have gotten a bit scared when almost bumping into him as well. However, she was now smiling towards Shade. "Good morning." Said Nemi with her usual sweet and innocent tone. Shade smiled back at her, he did not know why but he just felt so good that the first person he was able to see was Nemi. However, Shades mood dropped quickly after remembering that this might very possibly be the last morning he will ever see Nemi. Shade remembered how Daxyz had told him what was happening, he had no decision over Nemi staying or not. He felt even worse than before now. Nemi was still smiling very brightly towards Shade. Shade could not understand why Nemi was so cheerful. Shade was glad that Nemi wasn't sad about leaving, however deep down he felt a bit sad himself that Nemi wouldn't be even slightly upset about leaving. Shade spoke in a very soft voice, "So you think Daxys plan is really that great?" Nemi smiled once more when hearing him as she replied in her usual tone, "Oh so he told you? Yea I don't know why but he insisted on telling you about the plan himself. But yea the plan is really great isn't it?" Shade's expression dropped when hearing this. He thought maybe he wasn't seeing something but it looked very clear that Nemi had no problem with leaving. Shades voice was slightly shaky as he began to reply, "Yea.. I suppose it really is great... I just thought that.." Shade was interrupted by Daxys loud voice calling from the main living room. His tone was loud and firm as he spoke, "Hey the plan is starting now, if you have anything to talk about now is work time so talk about it later." Shade and Nemi both listened to Daxys as they walked to the room he was calling from. Shade however felt slightly uneasy, he knew that he might not even have a chance after this mission to talk to Nemi. However, he knew he did not have time to think about things like that. Daxys started to explain the mission without wasting any time. His voice was very stern as he explained the plan, "Alright guys, our main job is to get Nemi to the airport without any Rags interference." He nodded towards Nemi as he continued speaking, "However even if the Rags don't know about our plans it doesn't mean we won't encounter any. Therefore, extreme precautions have been taken. There will be three Golds cars for this mission. The drivers for those three cars will be myself, Albert, and Shade." When hearing this Shade looked up from the floor slightly. Daxys continued speaking, "Nemi will be in one of those cars heading to the airport. The other two cars as to not be noticed will follow the main car by driving on parallel streets. Bia will be giving directions as she keeps track of the mission from here by using her laptop." Shade looked at Bia and noticed she was wearing a headset with her laptop placed right beside her ready to start. Daxys then finished speaking, "Alright guys the flight leaves in exactly two hours so we better get moving, Shade and Albert go outside and wait in the cars." Shade could not help but feel that everything was moving too fast, he wanted to at least say bye to Nemi before starting the mission. He still slightly hoped that at least he would get to talk to Nemi while they drove to the airport. If he even was the person assigned to drive her. The boys walked outside in front of the house to where the cars were parked. Shade could notice Nemi and Bia hugging and saying their good byes right before leaving, he couldn't hear what they were talking about but could tell that Nemi seemed genuinely upset to be leaving. This made Shade begin to think of many things. He thought that Nemi was sad about leaving, just not sad about leaving him. This made him feel even worse but he once again did not say anything. When Nemi walked outside she was by herself, Bia must have turned on her laptop and was already starting her part of the mission. Nemi walked up to the boys and smiled. Nemi said her goodbyes to Albert and Daxys however did not mention Shade. Albert and Daxys then got into a different car each. Albert drove off ahead of everyone. Daxys stayed back to tell Shade they were going on ahead before driving off himself. The next thing Shade noticed was that him and Nemi were now completely alone with only one car left. Shade noticed that Nemi seemed to have gotten a lot quieter now. He really could not understand, she was cheerful and nice before but now she was just acting cold towards him. Was she that upset that he was the one who had to drive her? However, Shade still said nothing. They had both gotten into the car and began to drive to the airport. He could not see Albert or Daxys but knew that they must be somewhere near. He then realised that he did not have a phone of any kind on him, if something did happen how would Daxys and Albert know he needed help? Bia could see him on the GPS if his car stops moving but that wouldn't help very much. He was slightly worried but just hoped that nothing would happen. The first part of the trip was relatively quiet. Shade decided to try and talk to Nemi about what was happening one more time. He spoke in a pretty calm tone, "So is there anything you will miss about this place?" Nemi nodded and smiled slightly as she spoke in what seemed like a slightly sad tone, "Of course I will, I wish I didn't have to leave anyone I met here." Shade seemed puzzled to hear that answer as he replied, "But earlier you seemed so cheerful? I kind of thought you didn't really mind having to leave." Nemi then smiled softly as she shook her head slowly. "I know I'm sorry I shouldn't be like this but I just can't help feeling sad whenever I think I'm leaving. Even if it is for only..." Nemi was interrupted suddenly as the car behind them had just rammed into the back of Shades car. Shade knew that what happened was not an accident. He got so furious as he pressed down as hard as he could on the gas pedal and started to blaze down the street. Shade was angry not only because his car got rammed but mainly because he really wanted to hear what Nemi was just about to say. However Shade had to focus on losing the other car first. However, no matter how fast Shade went he noticed the car behind them still tailing them very close. "Damn it" mumbled Shade as he continued to try and lose the car following them. The only thing that Shade found strange is that the car behind them had not started shooting after them yet. Rags usually don't think twice about who they kill. The car following them was slowly getting closer and closer. Shade knew that the car following them was better than his so if things kept going this way he had very little chance of getting away. Shade continued to try and escape but now noticed that the other car was now merely inches away from the back of his car. Shade thought that he would probably get rammed again soon. "Hold on tight!" Shade called out to Nemi a moment before an incredibly loud crashing noise was heard. Nemi had her eyes closed at the time not knowing what was about to happen. She expected to feel some kind of pain after hearing a crash that loud however she felt nothing. She opened her eyes to see Shade still driving normally down the road. However, his expression seemed very surprised. Nemi quickly turned around to look out the back window. She could see a huge car pileup behind her. The car following her was one of the few cars that crashed. Also, one of the other cars that crashed looked exactly like the one Shade was driving, meaning that they were both just saved by either Daxys or Albert. Nemi squinted slightly but could see a hand sticking out of the car that looked exactly like Shades car. A smile spread across Nemis lips as she saw that hand giving the thumbs up symbol. Nemi and Shade both began to laugh after that happened, they spent the rest of the time driving to the airport while talking about how awesome their little adventure just was. They both seemed so happy while talking with each other. However, as soon as they reached the airport the thought of Nemi leaving made both of them get very quiet once again. It's as though neither of them wanted to admit that this was good bye. Nemi however did not seem as sad as before. She was actually smiling so at least Shade was happy to see that. It was pretty much completely quiet until Nemi got to the take off gate. Shade looked around quickly before speaking in a calm tone, "Are you sure you will be okay? There are people waiting for you as soon as you get there right?" Nemi still smiling nodded silently without saying a single word. Shade really did not know what to say now. He got her to the airport, his job was done, now was pretty much when they said good bye, but he just couldn't bring himself to say it. However, after taking a deep breath he began to speak, "Well... I guess this is good b..." Shade was not even able to finish his sentence before Nemi began to cry spontaneously out of nowhere. Shade was almost shocked when seeing this, he spoke in a caring tone, "What's wrong? You seemed to be..." Shade once again was interrupted in mid sentence as Nemi quickly embraced him without saying a single word. She held on to him very tightly and mumbled quietly, "I don't want to leave, I want to stay here. With you." Tears were still running down her cheeks as she talked. Shade was shocked. He slowly wrapped his arms around her as well and held her very close. He spoke in a very kind tone, "But earlier today... I actually thought you wanted to leave." Nemi sniffled slightly still holding on to Shade as she replied, "I'm sorry I know your probably disappointed." Shade now was even more confused, "Disappointed? About what?" Nemi sniffled once more, "Daxys told me last night that I shouldn't act sad around you today. He said that if I'm only leaving for six months you would think I'm silly for getting sad over that." Shade was now extremely confused. He however heard something that he needed to find out more about right now. He spoke in an almost unbelieving tone, "Six...months...?" Nemi nodded as she replied while still holding on to Shade, "Daxys wanted it to be a year but Bia convinced him that if I stay there for six months it should be long enough for the Rags to stop looking for me." Shade could not believe what he was hearing, slowly everything began to make sense. Shade then spoke in a quiet tone, "How come I was not told about this part of the plan?" Nemi when hearing this pulled back from Shade slightly and had a puzzled expression on her face as she spoke in her usual tone, "What do you mean? Daxys told you didn't he? I even remember last night Daxys asked if he could be the one to tell you." Shade nodded slightly and looked in a different direction as he spoke in a quiet tone, "Well... He did, to a point I guess... It's just..." Shade began to blush slightly while still looking away, "When he told me, I was under the impression I would never see you again..." Nemi looked up at Shade with wide eyes when hearing this, she was quiet for several moments before she began to giggle softly. She was worried the entire day because every time she looked at Shade he seemed to be so out of it. It made her blush a bit as well when realising that was what Shade was thinking about. She embraced Shade once more before letting go and stepping back slightly. She smiled once more and spoke in her usual tone, "I'm just glad this happened before I had to leave. That's all I care about." Shade nodded slightly. Before he could reply a message started to echo all throughout the air port saying "Flight Number 45661 departing soon." Nemi's smile seemed to drop a bit when hearing this as she spoke once more in a very quiet tone, "Well that's my flight... I should probably get going now." Shade nodded slightly before smiling warmly and reply with a very kind tone, "I hope you have a good flight." Nemi then nodded and smiled back before turning around and heading towards the entrance to the plane. Shade's smiled dropped as he watched her leave, he sighed softly as he turned around himself and started heading towards the exit. He seemed sad for some reason, he really didn't imagine it ending this way, even if he knew now it was only for six months. He was planning to go to a pay phone and call Daxys as he heard a voice calling his name from behind him. He turned around to see who it was and was surprised to see Nemi running towards him. She quickly without saying a single word wrapped her arms around his neck and kissed him very passionately. She let go after several moments and stood there before him. Shade tried his best to say something but he really had no words for the scenario he was in. Just as he was about to say something however the intercom came on again and said, "Final boarding call for Flight Number 45661" Nemi then smiled once again, "Sorry to just do that and run but my flight is leaving now, see you in six short months Shade!" And without another word she was gone. Shade actually stayed at the airport after that until he saw her flight leave. There were hundreds of thoughts going through his mind, so many that he actually decided to just stop thinking about anything all together. He walked out of the air port to where he had parked his car and to his surprise he saw Daxys leaning against his car. An almost diabolical smirk spread across his lips as he spoke in a very smug tone, "So? How did it go." Shade was able to connect almost everything together now, he knew that Daxys purposely didn't tell him that Nemi would leave only for six months knowing exactly how he would react. Shade walked up to him with a slightly angry glare, "You're an ass, do you know that?" Daxys chuckled for several moments and replied, "Yes yes. You and Bia always remind me." Shade sighed slightly as he spoke, "You're lucky it all worked out or I would hate you so much more right now." Daxys chuckled once again, "Yea I noticed, and in the middle of an airport too, nice one bro." Shade blushed a bit when hearing this as he spoke in a very defensive tone, "How do you know that?" Daxys replied with a chuckle, "Because two youngsters making out in the middle of an air port is totally not obvious to see." Shade squinted his eyes slightly while getting into the car with Daxys as he spoke in a not very serious tone, "I really hate you sometimes dude." Daxys chuckled once more and replied in the same joking tone, "Back at you bro." And without another word they drove back to base, too see what adventure would happen next.

Printed in the United States
By Bookmasters